A Bayou Boys Adventure

Marsh Monster

Gregory E. Zschomler

eyrie press

This is a work of fiction. Names, characters, places and incidences either are a product of the author's imagination or are used fictitiously, and any resemblance to actual persons, either living or dead, business establishments, events, or locales is entirely coincidental or used fictitiously.

The moral right of the author has been asserted.

Cover and text art by Creativity-Unlimited.

Publish in cooperation with **eyrie press**, Vancouver, WA

a subsidiary of Creativity-Unlimited

ISBN-13: 978-1484952436ISBN

ISBN-10: 148495243X

DEDICATION

This book is dedicated to my lovely daughters Bethany and Keilah whose sense of adventure and belief in themselves is admirable.

Become involved in the preservation of the disappearing bayous:

http://www.bayoupreservation.org/default.aspx/MenuItemID/197/MenuGroup/Home.htm

ACKNOWLEDGMENTS:

Once again this book could not have come to fruition without the support and editing skills of Ruth Zschomler, my dear (soon to be MFA) wife of thirty years. A special thanks to the amazing (14 year-old) Hezekiah 'Eagle Eye' Zschomler for the final copy edit. I'd also like to acknowledge the help and imagination of my son Jeremiah and the encouragement of my 'bestest' friend, author Will Glessner. Finally to my other author friends Brock Eastman, James Rubart, Graham Salisbury and Matt Mikalatos for their example, inspiration and encouragement.

NOTES TO THE READER:

As you read this book you will likely come across unfamiliar Cajun or French terms (in *italics*), as well as other terms and quotes. Many are marked with an asterisk (*). These are defined at the back of the book in the glossary. Other terms you might have to look up in a dictionary (which never hurts for expanding your vocabulary). Most of the places mentioned within this story actually exist (though some poetic license has been taken by the author). If you ever plan to visit New Orleans, do look them up on the Internet.

What's YOUR next great adventure?

TABLE of CONTENTS

1 RUMOR HAS IT

"Whataya mean?" asked Dallas.

My dad, Sheriff James Meyers, drove the rental van down Hwy 59/20 just south of Birmingham, Alabama. A gentle hum from the tires on the pavement came in through the windows, which were cracked to let in an evening breeze—a futile effort to quell the persistent southern heat and humidity. Dad was into fuel economy and only used the AC on rare occasions—like on days when people were known to spontaneously combust, which is extremely uncommon.

"I mean…well…I don't know what I mean," he said looking at us in the rearview mirror. "That's just what the reports are saying."

"You're telling me," I wiped the sweat from my forehead with my T-shirt sleeve, "that now the reported sightings of a 'swamp monster,'" indicating quote marks with my fingers, "are more frequent and..."

"Yes, Pete, it appears so."

* * *

I know, weird conversation, huh? I can explain. My dad's a parish* sheriff in southern Louisiana. My best friend is Bart Davis; his dad is a game warden. We often work together to solve mysteries. Kinda crazy for a couple of 16 year-olds, huh? However, just now we, along with a group of friends, were on a trip home from Washington D.C. and Langley, Virginia. We'd been up to the capitol to attend Acquire the Fire*—an awesome youth event—and we'd had the opportunity to tour the White House and CIA Headquarters.

We'd been invited by the President (that's right, the head honcho of the United States of America) after Bart and I had uncovered and thwarted a biological terrorism plot [that we called Voodoo Virus*] in the bayous* near our hometown of Houma, Louisiana. This trip had been kind of a reward. Anyway, this new conversation? Well, I think we're about to get involved in another mystery.

* * *

Anyway, my girlfriend Carla sighed, crossing her arms. I put my arm around her and pulled her closer, away from Reed who was sleeping with his head against the van's window, drool seeping out of the corner of his mouth. Bart's dad, Warden Davis, turned from his captain's chair on the passenger side of my dad, and assured, "I just need to stop in at Honey Island Swamp and see what's up, okay?"

Reed sucked in on his drool with a snort and a twitch. "Ewh!" exclaimed Carla, leaning away from him. I chuckled and, lifting my hand from Carla's shoulder, smacked Reed on the back of his head.

"Aliens!" awoke Reed with a start. Everyone laughed. Reed, even more of a geek than my fiend Bart and I, was known for his obsession with UFOs and other odd non-existing things, like zombies, vampires, ghosts and werewolves. I think he watches way too may reruns of *The X-Files* on Netflix.

"Another nightmare?" asked Keilah, poking him in the back from the seat behind.

"Ah, yeah," Reed answered, rubbing his eyes, "I guess so." Everyone laughed again as Reed looked around furrowing his brow.

"We were talking about the Honey Island Swamp Monster," I offered.

"Oh yeah," said Reed, "they're probably aliens."

"Probably," chimed Beth from the back seat with a wry smile and a roll of her eyes. Everyone laughed again.

"You're crazier than a fox in a hen house," said Dallas in his southern drawl. (His real name was Travis.) He was our newest friend and a recent Louisiana transplant from rural Texas. He was always saying hick stuff like that.

"Look who's talking about monsters, cowboy," retorted Reed.

"T'ain't no such thang, nor little green men, flyboy."

"Might be, ya know."

Dallas guffawed and Dad piped in. "This probably has whole lot more to do with earthlings than extraterrestrials," he said, "and nothing to do with monsters either, in spite of the myths."

"Even though such rumors have been floating around since before the infamous Harlen Ford sighting in 1963*." added Bart's dad, "Besides there's never been any *real* evidence—everything that was said to be 'evidence' turned out to be a hoax."

"But, that's the strange thing about that digital picture a tourist snapped last week," replied my dad. "It was still on the camera; no Photoshop involved."

"The marsh monster was photographed!?" mocked Keilah, "Again? Oh my goodness! So what? There are lots of supposed pictures and plaster casts of footprints."

"Marsh Monster," Reed pondered, "I like that." I thought of *The Creature from the Black Lagoon* (which I've seen like ten times).

"Doesn't surprise me," said Beth, turning to Keilah next to her. "What? Pictures in comic books?"

"No, seriously," continued Keilah, "they're at the paranormal museum."

"Yeah," I replied, "and fuzzy pictures of ghosts and zombies; and they're all over the Internet, too, but that doesn't mean…"

"That they're real," Keilah cut me off. "I know. That's what I'm saying."

"This one, they tell me, looks pretty convincing," assured Bart's dad. "It was taken with a professional camera, quality zoom lens and all, at 2400 dpi."

"Not even very blurry," added my dad, "even though it was taken from a moving airboat—which *was* full of eye witnesses, by the way. Saw the picture last week before we left. Awfully clear. Looks like a genuine Bigfoot to me—more organic than synthetic. But that doesn't mean it's not a fake.

"Oh, it's a fake," said the warden, "no matter what it looks like. Even though every neck of the woods—or swamp—has its legends, there's never been convincing proof that there's any kind of cryptid in existence."

"Cyptid?" questioned Bart, rubbing his temple.

"From the Greek *krypto* meaning 'to hide.'" Reed instructed, "It's a creature—or plant—whose existence has been suggested, but is unrecognized by scientific consensus, and often regarded as highly unlikely, though it's possible...if it hides."

"Where do you get this stuff?" I exclaimed.

"Wikipedia."

"You are *such* a geek, Reed," said Bart kind of cranky-like. Reed shrugged his shoulders and leaned once again against the door. We'd spent half of last night talking into the wee hours of the morning too hyped up on the concerts and Mt. Dew to settle down. Bart was probably tired.

"Wikipedia," mumbled Carla laying her head on my shoulder. It'd been a long weekend—too many late nights and early mornings—so I tilted my head to hers and closed my eyes with visions of Krypton—The Man of Steel's (a.k.a. Kal El's, a.k.a. Superman's) home planet. Cryptid, Krypton—they kinda sounded the same.

We were still a couple hours from home, but we had one more overnight stop to make—so we thought. We were planning on a brief stay in New Orleans, followed by a morning of sightseeing before heading home in the late afternoon. None of us got up to NOLA* often and so some rubbernecking was okay by us. There's always so much to see and do. And the food—not to mention the music—is absolutely to die for. But for now, well, it was time for a nap and that's what I did.

2 A CHANGE OF PLANS

Dad's cell phone jingled to the tune of *Dixie* and I awoke just as he said, "Jim Meyers." I listened in, hearing only his side of the conversation. "Yeah, yeah, okay. (pause) Oh really? (pause) Hmm, sounds interesting. (pause) Yeah, sure. Later. (pause) I'll call you when I get there." He hit the *end call* button on the face of his smartphone with a sigh and looked at Warden Davis. *Now what?* "Looks like they've got a possible 10-65, Bob."

I knew what that meant: a missing person. Not usually a big deal. Sometimes, sure, but most people show up sooner or later—and when they do, more often than not, alive and well. That is unless you're a kid. Missing kids, well, let's just say if you're a kid you don't want to go missing. Stranger danger and all that.

"Yeah?" said Warden Davis.

"Tour guide was a no-show for his shift a couple days in a row."

"What? And I suppose they think he got eaten by the swamp thing?"

"I'll, ah," Dad looked over the car seat, back at eager eyes and ears, "I'll fill you in on the details later." Bart's dad nodded.

This was getting weird. First, a week ago we hear about the rash of sighting incidents. Then someone snaps a picture and sends it to Bart's dad only hours before we leave on our trip. Next my dad hears about a "coincidentally" timely lecture on cryptids slated at the University of New Orleans offered by a renowned expert, Dr. Roberto Thachne.

Why the lecture now? I'm thinking this through, see. *Probably had a lot to do with people's curiosity about the recent sightings. A university has to take an active role in response to such things for marketing reasons, I suppose.* And now a mysterious disappearance. My interest was definitely piqued.

Bart, Reed, Beth and I had all wanted to attend the lecture, but now I was having second thoughts. I was getting more interested in what was actually happening down in the swamp. The others—Carla, Keilah and Dallas—could care less about the pontifications of some pompous professor and wanted to pass on the lecture altogether. "Hey!" exclaimed

Dallas, "I've never been down to Honey Island Swamp, could we, like, take one of those airboat tours?"

"Yeah," piped in Keilah, "me neither. Sounds like a great way to kill some time while you guys are at the lecture."

"Well," replied Dad, "I was wondering what you might want to do while we're helping out with the investigation. I think that would be fine. In fact, better yet, I think we could all go after the lecture. What do you think Bob?"

"Why not?" said Warden Davis. "It could be quite educational. Give the kids something to write about for school."

"I think we've still got enough in the kitty for a charter," said Dad. "I got better fuel economy on the trip than I expected." *Probably due to trying to steam us to death by not using the AC.* In fact, the van was beginning to smell like a sauna, which sort of smells like a gym locker the morning after a big game: rather robust.

"Awesome!" interjected Bart, obviously talking about the swamp tour and not writing a paper. Many of our folks—Bart and mine especially—were always on the lookout for 'educational opportunities.' That was part of our everyday life since many of us were home-schooled. It was kind of a plus and a minus, if you know what I mean. Keilah let out a little squeal and tossed her curls about. Dallas groaned. He was smart, but he wasn't keen on writing papers either. I mean who is, huh? We were already scheduled to write about the Langley and DC experience. Wasn't that enough torture? At any rate, we all agreed to write a paper in exchange for another adventure. Bribery, that's what I call it.

* * *

We pulled into New Orleans an hour and twenty minutes later and nearly forty-five minutes after that found a standard grade hotel with vacancies near the university. Finding a room in the Big Easy* can be more difficult than you might think; the city always seems to have some sort of festival going on, so tourists can overtake the available lodging rather quickly. Even though it was late in the summer, this was one of those occasions.

We unloaded our luggage from the van while my dad checked us in. By the time we lugged the luggage into the lobby we had assigned rooms so we all crowded into the elevator and rode to the third floor. "Man, I can't wait until tomorrow," said Keilah bouncing on her toes, "it's gunna be sooo cool!"

"I can," Bart yawned. "I'm bushed."

"Figure of speech," said Keilah as we reached our floor and the elevator door dinged opened. "I could use a couple z's myself."

“I’m so tarred I could sleep in the saddle,” said Dallas sauntering bow-legged down the hotel corridor.

“I’ll settle for a bed,” said Bart. In our rooms—a two room, three bed (plus futon) suite for the boys next to an adjoining double queen room for the girls—we unpacked what we needed for the night and got ready for bed. It was 11:42 when we finally hit the lights and the hay.

I dreamed I was at Acquire the Fire right in the middle of the Third Day* concert. The fog wafted (I love the smell of fog juice), the colored lights flashed, beams swung about the arena and the crowd went wild in worship. There was such a sense of God in the place.

The band segued from *God of Wonders* to *Kicking and Screaming* as the woofers thumped so hard you could feel it altering your heartbeat. Then the lights went to midnight blue and a sudden chill filled the air. I noticed that the crowd control security personnel were clothed in black suits. They wore shades and had little swirly ear bud wires running down into the collars of their shirts. They looked exactly like some of the CIA agents I’d met in Langley.

Then, seemingly out of nowhere, zombie hordes began shambling toward me. Panicked, I turned to run, but found myself hemmed in by the crowd. No one else seemed to see the beasts except the crowd control agents who also began to converge upon me. I struggled to disappear into the crowd, but could not. The first zombie reached out and grabbed me. I tried to fight him off as others joined their kind. I was grabbed by the hair and a bloodied open maw moved in toward my neck for the kill. But, instead of biting me, the creature jerked and slumped to the floor. He'd been shot in the head by one of the agents. I looked at the agent and saw white wings on his back.

I awoke and thought of how the dream had come together. I'd been to Acquire the Fire and I'd been to CIA headquarters. I got that. Then I thought back to how just weeks before Bart and I had thwarted a biological terrorism plot that involved zombies and a Voodoo Virus.

Okay, just my thoughts running wild. *But, was God trying to tell me something?* Had I any idea what I was in for, you would have had to drag me kicking and screaming into it. But Jesus had been with us through it all. No, I was safe in His arms and nothing—not even the hosts of hell—could drag me away from Him. I'd go anywhere with Him or for Him.

3 THE BIG EASY

At 9:30 a.m. the bedside alarm went off and we arose in various stages. Bart and Dallas being the early riser types, were up first. Reed and the girls dragged themselves out of bed reluctantly. Me? Well, let's just say I *did* get up. By 10:30 we'd showered, dressed and repacked, then went down to the lobby and followed the scent of baking Belgian waffles and fresh-brewed coffee to the dining room for a breakfast buffet that was included with our short stay. I thought of Dallas when my mind mused *I'm so hungry I could eat a horse*.

The morning news was on the eating area's flat screen as we filled our plates from the assortment of fruit, baked goods, oatmeal, biscuits and gravy, yogurt, toast and other fare. The weather report called for a decent late summer day. We made chit chat while we ate, otherwise not paying a lot of attention to the usual news of a big city crime and culture.

Just as Bart was filling a new plate with thirds the newscaster said: "This just in, the Honey Island Swamp Tours*..." Our attention was caught up by the report. Bart stopped mid-dollop in filling the Belgian waffle iron. "...have been suspended. Owner Jeb Plouet said that the recent disappearance of a local man caused the parish sheriff to call for a temporary closure of the popular tourist attraction while an investigation is underway. Here's Gina Boyer live on location at Honey Island Swamp Tours. Gina." Her image came on the screen and after a short pause she began.

"Yes, Mike. I'm here at Honey Island Swamp with Jeb Plouet. Jeb, anything to this swamp monster?" The camera zoomed out and panned for a two-shot.

"No, Gina," said the salty looking Cajun* man, "I been runnin' dis here operation for pert near t'irty years and I ain't never seen such a beast. Don't mean it don't exist, mind you. Dat's part of da mystery dat brings folk out here. We all keep our eyes peeled dough."

"What about the disappearance of tour guide Hap Deveaux?" said Gina. "He lives out in the swamp doesn't he?"

"Yup, lived out here goin' on twelve year. One a our guides he was...is. Hasn't showed up for work for two day. I went out dere to his place myself. Not hide nor hair of him. Boat's still docked, too."

"Any signs of foul play?"

"I didn't see none, and police ain't said anyt'ing neither."

"So how will this closure affect business?"

"On da one hand dis ain't really da big tourist season, so, normally, it wouldn't affect us all dat much. On da other hand dere's a boon in interest due to the rash of sightin's, so folk is wantin' to come out, 'specially since da weather is nice an' all. So, yeah, it's affectin' da bonus business we could have had had da cops not closed us down. Government meddlin' is what it is. A fella can't…" Gina turned to the camera as she brought the mic back to her mouth and the shot zoomed in on her.

"Thank you, Jeb. That's Jeb Plouet, operator of the Honey Island Swamp Tours, who's business has been suspended while the parish sheriff investigates the disappearance of, Hap Deveaux, a local man and tour guide. I'm Gina Boyer for Channel Four News. Back to you, Mike." The studio shot showed anchor Mike Metcaff at the news desk.

"Just a moment, Gina," said the anchor. "Have you spoken with local authorities about the disappearance?" Gina's image appeared in a box over his shoulder and then it zoomed out to fill the screen.

"I did attempt to speak with Sergeant Frank Rubart of the Saint Tammany Parish Sheriff's Department, but he declined to comment." The screen went to a divided shot with the studio on the left and the field shot on the right. "He simply stated that an investigation is underway."

"Thank you, Gina. The screen filled with the studio shot. "In other news…" he blathered on about a local bar fight. The waffle iron dinged and Bart looked down to see that the opened device held a half-cooked waffle—gooey on the top side.

"I guess that shoots our swamp tour," said Dallas.

"Not necessarily," said my dad. "I'm pretty sure I can still get us a charter. I'll speak with Sargent Rubart and, if there's no perceived danger, I can take you kids out with me." We finished our breakfast, went back up to our rooms for our bags, checked out and loaded into the van while Dad made a phone call to the local Cop Shop. Hanging up, he said, "Looks like we're good to go. There's no expected threat, and they're about wrapping up what they can concerning the missing persons investigation."

* * *

New Orleans, or 'Nahlins' as some of the locals say, is the biggest city in Louisiana, but *not* the state's capitol. You've probably heard of it in regards to hurricanes though; a few years back it was hit by a whopper called Katrina. The city is still recovering, but looking good in most areas. Since the lecture was at 1 p.m. we still had some time to gallivant around the city a bit and take in the sights. We would be heading out to Honey Island Swamp after attending the lecture; we had a 4:30 appointment for our private charter.

"Hey," said Keilah, thumbing the screen on her iPod Touch, "guess what Keilah's listening to." She began crooning a few bars from the song blasting into her skull through the earbuds jammed in her auditory canals. "God, I've fallen to my knees, I'm..."

"*Complete*, by Kutless," said Beth.

"Correct," said Keilah, she again thumbed her iPod and sang, "This too shall pass, oh. But it always comes knocking…"

"*Leap of Faith*, Sanctus Real," said Bart. One for Beth, one for Bart.

"Okay," said Keilah searching for another song. "What about this?" She pushed play and warbled, "Just a small town girl…"

Dallas jumped in, "Journey, cool. Our worship band did that song in church last Sunday. *Don't Stop Believing*."

"In church!?" asked Beth.

"Yup, listen to the lyrics, dude. Ah, dudess. It's about lonely, searching people. The sermon was about finding something to believe in." *How progressive*, I thought.

* * *

We swung by the university and, after getting directions at Administration, we tooled into the lot adjacent to the biology building to make sure we knew where it was before heading downtown.

"Can we stop by Café du Monde for some beignets?" asked Carla.

"Aren't you full from breakfast," I questioned.

"Never too full for beignets," she answered. It never ceases to amaze me how that girl can be so thin and eat so much.

"What's a bin-yay?" drawled Dallas.

"Dude! You've never had a beignet?" Carla looked shocked. "It's only the most delicious pastry in the world. It's a French-Acadian thing. You have *got* to try some."

"Pastry?" he said, curiosity and appetite piqued, "I'm game."

"Might as well," Dad piped in. "I was going to swing us by Jackson Square anyway. It's right across the street."

"Then can I check out the Faulkner House Bookstore?" asked Bart. He liked to read, and the used book store was a great place to catch some classics for a reasonable price. The book store use to be the house where author William Faulkner* lived and wrote.

"If you can make it snappy," said Bart's dad. "We know how you and book stores are."

The city's French Quarter was alive with street musicians—drummers pounding out syncopated staccato riffs on pickle buckets, sax players belting out the blues, jazz trumpeters doing their best to wail like Satchmo*, and small bands or duos playing everything from energetic Folk and Country to lively Dixieland and Zydeco* tunes—all with their tip jars prominently before them, bananas hanging on the rims. (I don't know why and I've never asked.)

There were street musicians and living statues, artists showing and selling paintings and jewelry, fortune tellers and panhandlers. A few ladies strolled the streets sporting frilly, pastel-colored parasols*, but most people looked like every day touristy types. The lingering scents of steaming gumbo, boiled crawfish, pan-frying pralines*, and freshly baked baguettes* wafted from restaurants that seemed to line every street. In fact each new block seemed come with its own café, bar and t-shirt shop. Lather, rinse and repeat.

Twenty-seven minutes later we had made it into the Big Easy and found a parking space near Pirate's Alley just south of Royal Rue* a block from the book store and just two from Jackson Square. Bart ducked into Faulkner's as we strolled into Jackson Square in front of the majestic, white-spired New Orleans Cathedral.

More street performers, artists and fortune tellers dotted the courtyard and we took time to watch and listen (to all but the soothsayers). When Bart rejoined us he had copies of Kate Chopin's *Bayou Folk and A Night in Acadie* and Mike Tidwell's *Bayou Farewell* under his arm and a tattered copy of Tennessee Williams' *Cat on a Hot Tin Roof* in his hand which he held out to me.

"This is for you, *padnet**. I know how you like the drama stuff. It was in the discount bin."

"Thanks, Bart," I said taking the script and tucking it into the back pocket of my jeans. "I've got the guts to die," I began, "What I want to know is, have you got the guts to live?"

"Huh?" said Carla.

"That's from *Cat on a Hot Tin Roof*," I said, "the play Bart just gave me."

"Oh," she rolled her eyes, "okay then." We wandered a few steps down Decatur to Café du Monde. The place, as to be expected, was busy and we stood in line for a seat.

"We've got less than two hours before the lecture kids," warned Warden Davis. "It's going to take thirty-five minutes to get back across town. We're going to have to eat and run, *if* we get in."

"We can hit the take-away counter," suggested my dad.

“Let’s do it,” said Carla. “I’m starving.” We snaked our way past the line of tourists and up to the take-away counter line (which was much shorter) and within minutes had our white paper bags of piping hot pastries. Our dads each grabbed a cup of chicory joe to go.

“Mmm, mmm,” said Dallas through a muffled mouth of beignet, powdered sugar smudged over his face and dribbled down the front of his western shirt.

“I told you they were yummy,” said Carla. We ate on our way back to the van and got inside. We’d saved some time by using the take-out so, with an hour to spare, Dad drove us through the Garden District—home of many Anne Rice Vampires.

* * *

In contrast to the French Quarter, the Garden District, with its Spanish moss*-strewn Live Oak* lined streets (pothole infested streets, mind you) was quiet and reserved. *How could these people in two to four million dollar homes put up with streets in such disrepair?* Here flower gardens and sprawling antebellum* mansions where everywhere. The perfumes of blooming flowers and fresh cut grass filled the air and contributed to a sense of relaxation.

“Wow, are these plantation homes?” inquired Dallas. Truly, this cowpoke hadn’t been out of Texas much.

"No," said Beth, "actually this multi-acre site *was* once a handful of sprawling plantations, but in the late 1800s parcels were sold off until, eventually, these antebellum mansions began to crowd in actually overtaking the gardens. It's now known more for its architecture."

"Wikipedia, right?" said Reed.

"Actually, I learned that from a travel guide."

"Actually," said Keilah, "you're a stickler for facts, actually." Beth gave Keilah a look and stuck out her tongue as Dad crept the van up to a stunning white mansion with a towering turret surrounded by a wrought iron fence.

"Beth is right though," interjected Bart's dad. "There are Victorian styles, Greek and Gothic…"

"I think we ought to head out," said Warden Davis. "Time's running short."

"*Fo troo**," answered my dad.

"What's that place?" I asked pointing at the white mansion.

"That," answered Bart's dad, "is the Davis House. And yes, my ancestors lived there. It was sold in 1955 during the war and later, in 1965, donated to the Women's Guild of the New Orleans Opera Association. The City later took over ownership and management of the place. They continued to lease it to the opera for thirty years operating under the Davis Playhouse name.

"And Pete, you may wish to know that they *did* produced shows there until last year when the City decided they could lease it for more money, raised their rent by a thousand dollars and, in essence, evicted them. It's said the place is haunted, too. Ironically, nobody has rented it since the opera moved out, until recently."

"Cool. Haunted." You guessed it; that was Reed talking with a glazed look in his eyes.

"A haunted opera house," I said, as the van moved on along the bone-jarring streets. "Original."

4 CRYPTOLOGY 101

Our group filed into the brightly lit lecture hall that seated over five hundred. It was mostly full. Many of the attendees appeared to be students dressed in sneakers, T-shirts and jeans, but there were also a number of older people, some dressed in suits and dresses, seated mostly at the back of the auditorium. Someone had set up a video camera behind the seating area and a screen near the podium was lit up from a video projector mounting to the ceiling.

We found seats three-quarters of the way from the front where we could sit together and sat down. The students spoke quietly amongst themselves, clicked open notebooks and shuffled papers for several minutes while others streamed in and found seats. The rich aroma of Starbucks lattes and mochas tantalized my nose. At precisely 1 p.m. a balding and bespectacled, chunky man rose from the front row and spoke into the podium microphone (it did *not* squeal nor did he tap it like in the movies).

"Students and esteemed guests, thank you for joining us today. For those who don't know me, I'm Professor Higgins, biology chair here at University of New Orleans. Today's lecture on cryptology will be given by visiting professor Dr. Roberto Thachne from the University of South Florida in Tampa. He's asked that I leave further introduction to him. My students will take notes and hand them in at the conclusion of the lecture. And, yes, they will count toward your grade."

Dr. Roberto Thachne met the department head at the podium, shook hands, and Professor Higgins took his seat in the front row as the visiting professor began his lecture.

"It is my pleasure to address you this afternoon as I hope it is yours," began Thachne clearing his throat. "I received my double Bachelors in history and biology from Cornell University, my Masters in biology from Yale and my Ph.D. in zoology from The Florida Institute of Technology.

"I might add that my dissertation on today's subject broke new ground and rocked the world of biology." It was clear this guy was full of himself. He reminded me of that puffed up villain in the movie, *Star Trek: Into Darkness*.

"Cryptology, or Cryptozoology as it is more accurateely labeled, is the study of cryptids—those plants and animals that science has yet to discover, but have, none-the-less, been discovered by non-scientists, that is the lay public. They are 'the hidden ones' which comes from the Greek kryptos, meaning 'to hide'." *Yeah, yeah, been there, done that.*

"I am the world's foremost authority on this science—though some in the science community don't see it as such—and I am dedicating my life to the discovery and documentation of these hidden creatures." A few hands went up around the room.

"You will hold your questions until the end of the lecture," snapped Dr. Thachne as hands slunk back down. "I'm sure I will answer most of them in the course of my discourse and I will not have you distracting me from my flow."

Bart rolled his eyes, "Wow!" he whispered. "He really thinks he's something."

"Now, the question of evidence, I'm sure, is foremost on your mind," continued Thachne, "but I will get to that. Be assured that, if there was not significant substantiation, I would be, as they say, just 'barking up the wrong tree,' but I am not." He pulled a small clicker device from his pocket and pointed it at the projector. An image of a hairy beast standing on two feet appeared on the screen.

"This," he said, now pointing the device at the screen and circling a laser pointer around the creature, "is the famed Sasquatch or Big Foot. This and other similar animals have been sighted in the Northwest United States and Southern Canada. A similar creature has been seen in the Himalayas and is known as Yeti or more colloquially as 'the abominable snowman;' no authenticated photograph exists." He advanced the slide.

"And this is the Loch Ness Monster, known as Nessy, sighted repeatedly in the Loch Ness of the Scottish Highlands. Also, this photo has not been authenticated. There *are* mysterious creatures on earth, of course, but here I segue from land-based cryptids to more water-based creatures. Here in Louisiana and the Florida Everglades you have…" He again advanced to the next slide. "… the swamp thing, the Honey Island Swamp Monster, the Creature of the Black Lagoon or whatever.

"This is the only known photograph of the Honey Island creature taken by a deer hunter in the area. Also not authenticated. And, of course, you have the 1960s sightings by Harlan Ford. The creature has been described as bipedal, seven or so feet tall, with gray hair and yellow or red eyes, and accompanied by a disgusting smell…" *Sounds like Bart.* "Footprints supposedly left by the creature have four webbed toes."

He advanced the slide. "This is a photograph of a supposed plaster cast of that footprint taken by Ford." He advanced the slide. "As you know, there has been a significant rise in the number of sightings lately and that is why I am here." So far, nothing new. My own thoughts began to wander and I looked around the room. I wasn't the only one. Several students seemed bored and were doodling, tapping pens and passing notes. My mind drifted to our upcoming Honey Island Swamp excursion. I wondered what I would see. *Would I see the swamp monster?* Dr. Thachne droned on:

"Cryptids are solitary creatures and do not wish to be found. They are not afraid of humans, they simply wish to be left alone and, when threatened, can be quite dangerous. In the case of the Honey Island bigfoot, I believe its habitat may be threatened. As the coastal land mass disappears and civilization continues to encroach upon these beings they are reacting.

"We talk about *the* thing when, perhaps, there are many *things*. We may be invading an entire species or tribe. It is our duty—our responsibility—to pull back and let them be. Now, you may be thinking: Why am *I* invading their space? The answer is that science also has the responsibility to know. I am a scientist—a biologist—and I seek knowledge. Knowledge is the greatest treasure we have." A hand shot up, but the speaker ignored it. "It is essential…"

The hand-raiser waved his arm in the air and said, "Excuse me." The professor looked sternly at the student, but continued. "It is *essential* that we document this..."

"Excuse me, sir, why is knowledge...?"

"I asked that I not be interrupted!" Thachne's face grew redder with every word he spoke. "What *you* have to say is irrelevant to the lecture. *I* am speaking here—I am the teacher and you are the pupil. Do you understand? Or are you stupid?" Wow! Talk about megalomaniacs. A hush came over the room. Thachne cleared his throat, shuffled his notes and finally continued. "Documentation is essential so that we understand our world and our place in it. There is nothing more valuable than knowledge and pursuit of knowledge is transcendent.

"Now, the existence of cryptids *is* factual. Numerous eye-witness reports verify this. Just because no one has been able to collect reliable physical evidence does not discount what is obvious. People have encountered these creatures and, even under hypnosis or monitored by polygraph, the truth is confirmed.

"So, since these creatures exist and wish to be left alone it is essential that we—and I mean professional scientists alone—cautiously and carefully explore their presence. You will note the reports of several 'ape-like' creatures that attacked a cabin in the Pacific Northwest by raining boulders down upon it. These creatures felt threatened. The same is true for the Honey Island Swamp Monster. The recent disappearance of this tour guide is a warning. Stay away. Let the professionals handle it. We will let you know what we find."

Blah, blah, blah. The lecture went on to describe the creature as a being capable of thought, possibly a cross between mammal and reptile and most likely living in families. With that he launched into a sermon about protecting one's young and how that was instinctive. He closed with another warning to remain out of the swamps—until he declared it safe—and ended on time without taking questions. *Figures.*

The room emptied to a dull roar of book gathering and idle chit-chat. "What a jerk," I whispered to Carla. My father caught the comment.

"What have I told you about judging others?"

"Sorry, dad."

"Do not speak ill of others," he said. "It only degrades *your* character." I looked sheepish as we returned to the car. *Sheesh!* The guy *was* a jerk. He seemed to care more about these creatures—*if* they even existed—or knowledge, than about people. I doubted he cared about anything, really, except himself. He was like some maniacal dictator—a drug dealer, a terrorist, a murderer. As far as I was concerned, these types of people were the scum of the earth, feeding off others without regard to how they hurt others. I didn't see any reason why such people deserved our respect.

5 DOWN ON THE BAYOU

"Do you think we'll see that marsh monster thing?" asked Keilah.

"Bigfoot," interjected Reed.

"Whatever," replied Keilah with a flip of her wrist.

"Probably not," said Warden Davis. "It's mostly been seen close to dusk."

We crossed the I-10 Lake Pontchartrain causeway (it's a bridge of sorts, only a few feet above the water and a creepy fourteen miles long) and turned toward the marshy expanse known as Honey Island Swamp. Located southeast of New Orleans, it's flanked on the north by I-90, on the south by Lake Borgne, on the east by the Pearl River and on the west by the West Pearl River.

"This is a lake?" questioned Dallas.

"Not really," answered Warden Davis. "It's really just a brackish estuary. It is, however, one of the largest wetlands in the world and covers an area of 630 square miles. The average depth is only about twelve to fourteen feet."

"It's like Texas big, dude," Dallas observed. We turned south toward Slidell.

* * *

The twisty-turny gravel road, led up to a large, mostly empty gravel parking lot. A small, weathering bungalow-type building with two rockers on the porch sat off to the side of the lot. A sheriff truck and a beat up Chevy half-ton were the only other vehicles in sight. The carved wooden sign on the building read *Honey Island Swamp Tours*. Another sign sporting a picture of an alligator read *Trespassers Will Be Delicious*.

The rhododendrons were in bloom—bright pink and red clusters against the deep browns and muted greens of the surrounding vegetation. Their fragrant perfume mixed with the pungent, earthy smells of the nearby swamp. Various rustic bird houses hung about the place.

Dad parked the van in the nearest non-handicap parking space and we piled out into the sunny-breezy weather. *Twee, twee, twee* called a bird. *Chur, chur, chur* answered another. The doors of the white, red lettered Saint Tammany Parish sheriff's truck opened and two officers stepped out sauntering our way.

"Afternoon," said my dad, walking toward them extending his hand, "I'm…"

"Yes, Sheriff Meyers," said a rather lean officer, extending his own hand. "We've been expecting you. Pleased to meet yer acquaintance. I'm Frank Rubart and this is Brock Eastbrook."

"Officer Rubart, officer Eastbrook."

"Call me Frank," said the lean man. "And he goes by B.D. as in beady-eyed." The other man didn't respond except to touch the brim of his hat. I suppose he was used to the remark.

"As long as we're on a first name basis, I'm Jim and the kids are…"

"Pleased to meet y'all," he said, tipping his Smokey Bear hat. "Yer tour guide can take y'all out to the Deveaux place. We've got it marked off with police tape. Yer free to explore the usual tour route, too—plenty of wildlife out there. And let us know if y'all see anything suspicious."

"Sure will," answered my dad "Thanks Frank."

"Jim," he answered, "y'all have a good time. Oh, he's my card; call my cell if ya need to."

Dad took the card, "Thanks Frank."

* * *

We moved into the tour-gift shop-café building, skirting past a lizard sunning itself on the railing, and met the man from the TV, none other than Jeb Plouet, standing behind the counter of the gift shop, snack bar and tour registration desk. The place was well stocked with plasticized alligator heads, souvenir visors and T-shirts, plush-toy alligators, rubber snakes, key chains, postcards, quick energy food and drinks and more. There were a few aquariums that held baby alligators and turtles near the door by a window.

Jeb looked thinner than he had on the tube, but was, none-the-less, a portly man dressed in baggy overalls, a rather large beige T-shirt and a wide-brimmed floppy tan hat. He smiled a toothy grin and stepped toward us. "Afternoon," he said, "ya must be my charter."

"That would be us," said Bart's dad.

"Well, we'd best git started den," Jeb said. Like most Cajuns he couldn't pronounce the *th* sound, so it came out like a *d*. "Daylight's a-burning. Normally, I'd charge ya twenty buck a head, but dis one on da house, beings as ya got a law officer with ya. Might help us find ol' Hal. He's my best friend in da world. Why he even...well, dat's a big story. Anyways, come on." He turned and sauntered out the front door over which hung a sign that read:

We followed. Outside the man indicated the camera hung around my neck, "Ya want ya picture taken?" He smiled, "Prove ya was here and gives us a record should ya go missin'." He grinned his toothy grin. I handed him my camera and we posed for a photograph in front of the carved sign that hung from the porch, then walked toward the boat ramp. Beyond a rustic wooden queue, covered in weathered canvas, was a dock and beyond that a dilapidated building that opened into the water—a shed for boat stowage I imagined.

Moored to the dock was a flat aluminum boat with bench seats running down the center which faced out to the sides; at the stern was a huge Yamaha 150 outboard motor. Jeb put one foot in the vessel and kept the other on the wharf. He assisted each of us onboard while he laid a few ground rules.

"Have a seat anywhere ya like, folks," said Jeb. "The coast guard requires dat I go over a few t'ings afore we git head out. Stay seated while da boat's in motion; please keep ya body parts inside da railing at all times lesson ya want to lose a finger to a gator; dere are lifejackets under ya seat should ya need dem. We'll be underway as soon as ya situated. Tank ya for joining us today at Honey Island Swamp Tours where adventure awaits—and so do hungry alligators."

It was a well-practiced spiel and sounded like one. Bart leaned over and told me he wondered if the remaining pitch would be as dull as this or if it would be more like the one-liners that peppered the Jungle Cruise at Walt Disney World. I half expected him to say, "Dis here is da wildest ride in da wilderness!" (which actually comes from the pre-ride at Big Thunder Mt. Railroad). Speaking of Disney World, I wished Will was with us. He wasn't. His family had planned their trip to the Magic Kingdom a year ago and there was no way he was going to miss it for our trip. Even though we'd had a blast, so far, I envied him. I hadn't been over to ol' WDW for five years.

When we were all seated Jeb started the engine. A black puff of oily gas exhaust blew over us, its nasty smell momentarily masking the floral scents of blooming flowers mixed with pine, and swamp. The water looked like strong coffee that had been well creamed as Jeb gingerly pulled away from the dock. "Folks, dis a wildlife management area regulated by state hunting and fishing regulations—including alligator coming up in September.

"We have turtles, alligators, great blue herons, egrets, wood ducks, teal, horned owls, deer, wild hogs, frogs and a wide variety of snakes—some venomous—out here. Below the surface dere are crab, shrimp, crawfish and sport fish—a lot of catfish and white perch. Da catfish are a commercial fish so dey're caught year 'round, the other species are regulated by season."

Jeb gunned the engine, did a quick cookie and we were buzzing into open water. The breeze was quite chilly. Within a couple of minutes he slowed the vessel for a marked *No Wake Zone*. Along the shoreline attractive homes dotted the wooded rises. Stilted shacks also stood on the water's edge, each sporting a dock. Some were in sad disrepair—never repaired or rebuilt since the Katrina storm surge wiped them out—others were quite nice. Several had stacks of crab traps standing next to them.

"Yup, people live out here year 'round in these camps, making a living at shimpin', crabbin' an' such," said Jeb now that the engine was idled down. "Others come down seasonally or on da weekends to fish and trap. Lots of nutria out here, too. Years ago seven came over from Vietnam and now da population runs close to twenty million. Dey kin have up to four litter a year and dey'll eat anything. Da game department pays five bucks a tail fer 'um.

"As ya kin see Katrina did a lot of damage here. Dere was a fifteen foot storm surge and if you look at dat dere house you can see da water line stain halfway up da side. Da water's a tad high right now, too. If it gits any higher I'm gunna hafta buy my chickens hip boots." He gunned the engine again and steered the vessel into a side channel, where he slowed once again to a crawl.

"A friend of mine operates anudder tour outfit. He fell outta his boat once and got a leg bit off by a gator. I called him in the hospital as soon as I got the news. 'Jeb,' he said, 'a gator bit off my leg.' I asked, 'Which one.' He said, 'I don't know, all dem gators be lookin' da same to me.'" I thought that was funny, but it only made Bart nervous; I could tell by the way he looked at me.

"Seriously, dis is a recreation area and people *do* waterski and swim out here as well as hunt and fish. I grew up here and did plenty of dat sort of t'ing, even dough, now as an adult, da idea makes my skin crawl—considerin' the snakes an' gators that make dis dere home."

"But dese bayas be disappearing. Evera year a chunk of sou'dern Louisiana equal to da landmass of da island of Manhattan is lost to da sea."

"Wait a minute," I interjected. "I thought that was a football field a year."

"Oh, no, no, no. Dat's per day, son—a football field evera day." I was dumbfounded. I lived here and had no idea. Our tour was fascinating. Bart and I had spent lots of time out in the bayous near home, but never had we marveled like this.

Sure there was the usual flora and fauna—magnolias and mangroves, gum trees, cedar, cypress and live oaks laden with gray Spanish moss, red leaf maple, Cherokee rose, duck grass, elephant ear and all kinds of animals. Oh! And bugs—*lots* of bugs.

We learned that the tannic acid in the water was what gave the second-growth *bos coya* their knobby knees; the first growth had been logged off. (We also learned that they were related to the redwoods of California and that they could live for nearly 2,000 years.) The pond lilies were in bloom—opened up to the afternoon sun with their yellow flowers. There were also plenty of snakes. We saw water moccasin, diamond backs, cotton mouths, rat snakes and more, all sunning themselves, entwined on branches just off the water's surface on up to ten feet or so. (Like Indiana Jones, I hate snakes.) We did see turtles and alligators, as well as all kinds of birds, too, including a large horned owl.

6 HAP'S PLACE

"Da Ocola Indians* lived along dese here banks for t'ousands of years. Oh, look over dere," Jeb said, gesturing. "You see dat dere purple flower? Dat's da Louisiana Iris also known as da *flue de luce**, which is da NOLA symbol and da Saints insignia. Da t'ree points dat stick up, dey represent da trinity. You recognize it? An' look, you can see a gator head over in dat algae. She's probably a seven-footer. If you can only see da head, you can still judge its length. Da distance from da eyes to da end of da snout in inches generally correlates to its body length in feet." That was new to me; handy information.

Twenty minutes later we pulled up next to Hap's camp where his boat was still moored. The place was quiet. Yellow plastic police tape warned *Do Not Cross,* but we did. (After all Dad was a cop.) Jeb stayed in the boat. "Don't touch anything," my dad instructed, "this might be a crime scene." Bart and I knew the drill. Been there, done that. Anything might be evidence.

"No touchy," I said in my best David Spade imitation.

"*The Emperor's New Groove*," Bart said, recognizing my quote. I smiled and nodded. The rustic building stood on stilts above the waterline. Unpainted and weathered, it looked like it had seen better days. It wasn't much bigger than my living room back home. Stepping inside we spread out and stood about gawking as our dads poked around. Though a bit unkempt, it didn't have that ransacked look you see in movies when bad guys are looking for something. You know, drawers spilled out, mattresses cut open, overturned furniture, stuff like that.

It just looked lived in by a bachelor; dishes piled on the counter, garbage not taken out, clothes on the floor, bed unmade. *Bart's room*, I thought The malodor was a bit pungent. *Yeah, definitely Bart's room.* A ceiling fan/light hung on over the sofa-bed and a hunting magazine lay on the nightstand next to it. Yeah, these places had electricity, but not plumbing. The bed appeared to have been slept in. "Looks like he might have been reading," said my dad, mostly to himself.

"Hmm," replied Bart's dad, still in deep thought. I wandered to the kitchen area that wasn't much more than a counter. I knew it was a kitchen area because it had a microwave, fridge/freezer and hotplate. There was no sink. The trash receptacle was near full—TV-dinner boxes and a two-liter soda bottle were on top—with a couple roaches crawling around. It appeared that he last ate a dinner of Salisbury steak (a.k.a. mystery meat), peas, mashed potatoes and brownie washed down with Mt. Dew. *Not into nutrition or gourmet cuisine, I guess.*

"Check this out," Beth was kneeling next to the left of the door jam.

"Whoa," exclaimed Reed, standing beside to her. All of us turned, looked and walked across the small room in their direction. Bart's dad, swung into full game warden mode.

"Don't touch it!" He knelt down and gazed at that the footprint on the floor.

"What is it?" I asked the question I'm sure we all had.

"What does it look like?" said Reed. "It's a footprint. A bare, large, muddy footprint of a four-toed swamp monster!" You could feel the air sucked from the room as everyone took a gasp.

"That," said Bart's dad, "is what you call jumping to conclusions." He whipped a small digital camera from his vest pocket (game wardens wore vests with lots of pockets) and snapped several photographs. "This is likely a hoax, a plant;

could be anything. Yeah, it's a print alright—might not be what it appears to be though." He bent closer and pointed at the side of the print. "Hair here. I need to get a forensic kit out here. You've got one at the office, don't you Jim?"

"Sure, but that's a couple hour's drive."

"Right. I'll call the Saint Tammany Sheriff and see if they've got one." He flipped his phone open, took the sergeant's card from his pocket and dialed. After a pause, while it rang through, he spoke with the officer and arranged for a kit to be picked up at the tour dock. He hung up with a snap, "All set."

"Good. Let's skedaddle back and snag that puppy, Bob. We've got an…" It was then we heard *it*. Whatever it was it sounded…it sounded…it was unearthly and hideous, primal and guttural—like no sound I'd ever heard before and I'd heard bobcat and boar, coyote and bear. I'd even heard Wookie, taun-tuan and sand people—in *Star Wars*—and this was *way* worse.

"Yikes!" said Reed. Warden Davis popped to his feet. Dad put his hand on his gun and the two of them spun to the door.

"Who says 'yikes'?" asked Beth.

"Reed says 'yikes,' answered Keilah.

"I say 'yikes' and 'let's git outta here,'" said Dallas. Our dads were on the porch looking every-which-way.

"You see anything?" Dad said to Jeb. The guide shook his head no.

"Nothing," answered Bart's dad. "Which way did the sound come from?" Jeb shrugged.

"No idea. Didn't notice," the warden hollered back toward where we stood in the doorway. "You kids have any idea which direction that sound came from?"

"East," I said. (I notice these things.) They strode to the edge of the porch railing on the east side and looked out into the darkening distance.

"See anything?" Dad looked back and forth at Warden Davis and Jeb.

"Nope," said Jeb, "but while dis ain't da first time I heard dat sound, I never heared it afore las' mont'. No idea what it is eder."

"Let's get the kids out of here," said Bart's dad, "and come back with that kit."

"Sounds like a plan. Come on kids, into the boat."

"But…" I said.

"No buts about it. This could be dangerous."

"Danger is my middle name," I tapped my chest.

"Peter, this is not the time to joke around." *Man, I love my pops, but he seems kind of cranky today. Does he have to ride me so, in front of my friends? So I'm not perfect. Who is?*

"Come on now. In the boat," ordered my dad. Within minutes we were underway and took a recon spin down an eastern running channel before giving up and tooling back toward tour headquarters. Our dads, sitting close in the back of the boat, talked with one another in as hushed tones as possible. Once back, Jeb pulled up to the dock, moored the boat, helped us out and walked us back to our van. "I hope da tour has been helpful," he said and then pointed over toward the boat launch. "Sherriff, if you're actually going back out dere, ya can use our airboat over dere. It's faster."

"That would be great," said Warden Davis. (That's what he used back in Houma.)

"I'll git da keys fer ya," and Jeb wandered into the tour shack as we stood around the vehicle making chit chat.

"I'll call Dolores and let her know of our plan," said Dad as he stepped away from us, taking the radio from his belt and calling into his dispatcher-office manager.

"That sound we heard out there," said Keilah, "it was spooky."

"And those tracks," said Reed, "I want to see the thing that made it."

"No, you don't," said Beth smiling. "It would probably suck you up to the mother ship, do a rectal exam, take your brain out through a straw, implant a chip in your nasal cavity, and take DNA samples from your spine with a super-charged Hoover." Everyone laughed as Reed turned a ghostly grayish white.

"On second thought," he said. (Told you he watched too many *X-Files*.)

Jeb returned momentarily. "Here," he said, "an' be careful. I'm goin' home, if ya need anyting' here's my number." Dad took the piece of paper he held out and Jeb looked us over. "All accounted for den?" We nodded. "Any fingers missin'?" We shook our heads. "Den it was a good tour." He chuckled and sauntered off toward a beat up Chevy truck that looked like it had seen better days. We got in the van, Dad started the engine and we tooled up the drive, Jeb right behind us.

7 MISSING

We'd taken a hotel room at a quaint graying roadside motel in Slidell and ordered in pizza from the gas station-convenience store-pizzeria down on the corner. Our dads were out to Hap's place with the borrowed airboat and a forensic kit. The hotel room was pretty quiet except for the sound of an occasional car passing by on the adjacent road outside, the pizza was cold and no one felt like talking. Our dads were running late. My cell phone rang and I answered. "Oh, Mom, it's you. We haven't heard from Dad yet."

"I know." She sounded like she had seen a ghost—or a swamp monster.

"What is it? Is it about Dad?" There was silence. "What is it?"

"I..I just got off the phone with Dolores," Her voice quavered. "There's no contact with your father. No radio…" she trailed off.

"He hasn't checked in?"

"Dolores can't reach him through either dispatch radio or by cell. There's no answer. Bob isn't answering either. It's been over an hour since they last talked."

"They said they'd be back about 'dark-thirty,' I said. "Maybe they're on their way and can't hear over the airboat's fan."

"It's well past dark and they'd be docked within twenty minutes. Dolores has dispatched a local search…"

"They need a rescue!?" My dad could be in danger, maybe even…dead. I swallowed hard. Yeah, my dad was a cop; he put his life on the line every day. It was something I had learned to accept. Mostly.

"Peter, don't worry, it's..."

"Why not? *You* are." Moms!

"Just hang in there. I'll keep you posted if I hear anything. You…you going to be okay?" I could hear the distress in her voice.

"What do you think?" I'd get through it, sure, but I felt pretty upset. I could feel the visceral tension welling up inside me.

"You kids hang in there. It's going to be all right."

"Sure, Mom." I thought of all kinds of things I wanted to say and ask, but I didn't need to give her any more anguish. "Love you."

"I love you, too." I hung up and looked at Bart.

"Our dads are missing."

Beth gasped and pulled her hands to her mouth. "I figured that," said Bart hanging his head. "Question is, what are we gonna do about it?"

"Oh, no, no, no, no," interjected Reed. "You are *not* going out there! I mean, you're not thinking of that…*are* you?"

"I am. I don't expect you guys to come; that wouldn't be good. You shouldn't. You won't, but…well, Bart and I *have* to."

"No, you don't," said Beth. "This is best left to the authorities."

"Our dads *are* the authorities and…"

"You *can't* go out there," said Keilah. "It's foolish."

"Look, it's not like we've never been out on a bayou in the middle of the night. We *did* undercover that Voodoo Virus thing," I assured.

"And you were shot, Pete!" said Carla. "You could have been killed."

"But I wasn't."

"What about *this* time?"

"Well," I couldn't help myself but quote *Star Trek's* Worf, "'today is a good day to die.'" She gave me a seething glare.

"Look, it's what we do, okay. Now let's get over it and get to formulating a plan." Bart and I were going out and there was no doubt about it—no debating the matter further—and everyone knew it. (We were pretty pig headed—especially Bart; he smelled like one, too.) What we *did* debate is the best course of action. Getting out there, what to take, what we could do, what we'd find. "We need some boom sticks," I said, thinking of what I'd heard about from *The Grey*—a movie I'd never seen due to its R rating.

"Where on earth are you," said Bart, "a sixteen year-old, going to get shotgun shells—especially this time of night?"

"Ah, yeah, right." My mind whirled. "I suppose C-4 is out of the question, too?"

Carla chuckled, "You are such a pyro!"

"Ya know," said Reed, draping his arm over my shoulder, "I used to be an adventurer like you, then I took an arrow in the knee." We were so ill-equipped. (Absolutely nothing explosive.)

* * *

"Tony Stark!" I said out of the blue.

"What?" asked Beth.

"Iron Man," answered Bart.

"Yeah," said Beth, "I got *that*."

"He's got a movie idea," said Bart. "And?"

"Iron Man three," I said, "when Tony didn't have a suit he could use he went shopping at the hardware store."

"Oh, yeah," said Keilah, "he bought stuff he could make weapons out of."

"Correct-a-mundo!" I said and followed up with a string of ideas. A minute later it was decided: we needed to get a taxi to a Home Depot for supplies. Carla went to work with the phone book she'd found in the hotel room's nightstand to find both. We decided we could borrow a tour boat when we got to Honey Island Swamp.

Carla insisted in the end that she would go with us, though I tried in vain to dissuade her. She said I wasn't going to go without her and that was that, so live with it. Reed was assigned our home base communications man—he had the only other cell phone among us, besides mine. Now for the details.

"How much money do we have?" I asked. "I've got about twenty-four fifty." Everyone dug into their wallets, pockets and/or purses and withdrew their cash and began counting while I took the hotel notepad and pen from the nightstand and wrote my sum at the top.

"I have fourteen dollars and seventy cents," said Beth.

"I have twelve thirty-five," added Carla. I wrote the amounts down in a column below my original entry.

"Fifteen bucks," said Dallas.

"Twenty-four seventy-two," said Reed.

"Two o' two," said Keilah, sheepishly. "I bought a few T-shirts at the event." Bart was still counting.

"And Bart?" I questioned.

"A hundred forty-seven forty-eight, and some change. One forty eight, fifty…four." All eyes were on him. After a moment he looked up and said, "What?"

"Dude! You've been putting fast-food away like Bill Murray eating breakfast in *Groundhog's Day*," I said. "And you *still* have more money than I started with."

"I came prepaid."

"I'll say," I said. "That's six weeks allowance for me."

"I've been helping the Carreire's with their net mending business."

"Kin I get a job with 'um?" asked Dallas.

"Maybe next year," answered Bart. "We're done for the season."

"Okay," I began totaling, "lessee."

"Two hundred thirty-nine eighty-three," Beth blurted.

"What?" Keilah asked. "You, like, added that in your head?"

"I'm good at math."

"She's right," I said. "Two hundred thirty-nine eighty-three on the nose. We've got about two hundred and forty bucks."

"Oh wait," said Dallas removing his Stetson. He flipped it over and withdrew narrowly folded and sweat-stained a hundred dollar bill from the band inside his sou'wester. Unfolding it he handed it to me. "Ma ropin' money."

“You’re what?” asked Carla.

“Ma winnin’s from rodeoin.’ I put it there cuz I weren’t packin’ ma wallet. Can’t ride a horse with a spur in yer saddle.”

“Yeah, okay,” I said, “we have about three hundred forty bucks. Now what?”

“Well, said Carla, “we’re gonna need flashlights and batteries.” I wrote that down. “How about some rope?”

“Rope,” asked Bart, “what for?”

Dallas spoke up, “Rope is good for lassos, towin’, tyin’, climbin’, bindin’, trippin’, hangin’, hitchin’ up yer pants, an’…”

“We *git* the idear, cowboy,” interrupted Reed. “You know ropes.” I wrote down rope and waited for more *idears*. None came.

“Anything else?” Silence.

“Ah, flares?” asked Keilah, “For signaling.” I wrote it down.

“Say, Pete,” said Bart, “I think you just need inspiration. You get to the hardware store and it will come to you.” *What do you get from a hardware store that will help you save your dad from who-knows-what out in a swamp?* I guess I would have to improvise.

* * *

My cell phone rang again and I fell upon it like I was trying to snatch a twenty dollar bill from a fire before it burned. "Mom? Dad?"

"It's your mom. I'm just checking up on you. See how you're doing before bed."

"Heard anything?"

"Nothing new. I called Dolores. She said the local sheriff team has come back in." I could tell from Mom's voice she was trying to be stoic. "They found…" I heard faint sobs on the other end of the connection. Then there was that question I couldn't ask. I couldn't ask if dad was dead, so I just sat there, listening.

"Peter, they found the boat and the forensic kit. They found…muddy footprints and…blood." She began to sob bitterly. I sat there in shock. If she was here she would come over to the bed, compose herself, sit down beside me and wrap her arm around my shoulders where we'd be a comfort to one another. But she wasn't here; I wasn't there. We were both alone in this. "It doesn't mean anything, it could be nothing." *Yeah, right.* "You going to be okay?" *Okay? Okay with my dad missing, possibly dead? Like, nooo.*

"You'll tell me if you hear anything?" I said, and then thought better of it; I didn't want her calling to find me gone.

"Better yet, I'll call *you* tomorrow. Don't want to wake the whole room."

"I haven't decided if I need to come out there yet. For now I'm going to monitor the situation through Dolores. They'll resume the search tomorrow morning. As long as your safe and sound, honey."

"Okay, Mom, we are. I better go. We're pretty bushed," I said, not wanting to out and out lie, saying we were going to bed when we weren't. And truthfully, we were feeling pretty wiped out. "I love you, Mom."

"I love you, honey."

"Goodnight," I said and hung up. I shook off the sadness in my heart by calling upon a memory verse: *"Why so downcast, oh my soul; put your trust in God.*"* I sent up a quick prayer, then struck a dramatic pose for quoting Shakespeare.

"'To woe the slings and arrows of outrageous fortune…to take arms against the sea of troubles, and by opposing them, end them…'"

"There he goes with *Hamlet* again," whispered Carla to Bart.

"I know, he's weird like that," he answered back.

"To task, my friends!" said I. *Said I? Maybe I am a nutcase.* I called the cab company.

8 PUTTING THE PLAN TOGETHER

Half-hour later Bart, Carla and I arrived at Lowe's (no Home Depot in town) an hour before closing with no real idea what we wanted beyond a couple of flashlights and flares...and some rope. We began systematically wandering the vast isles of hardware and home improvement supplies.

"Duct tape!" said Bart. "We need duct tape."

"What do we need duct tape for?" asked Carla.

"I prefer gaff tape," I said.

"What's gaff tape?" she asked.

"It's like duct tape only it's a theater or film tech's best friend," I answered. "Comes in matte black and comes off clean without residue."

Carla shook her head "Oh, cool. So, why do we need it?"

"I dunno," said Bart, "but either one can come in handy with over 1001 uses."

"Yeah, nice. What else?"

"How about a chainsaw?" I asked thinking about how they were used as weapons in various zombie and horror movies. "No, too grizzly."

"And too expensive," added Carla.

"Look here," said Bart, approaching an entire wall of hardware and wire of every size and tinsel strength. "We could use some wire for trip lines with those screw eyes between two trees."

"Hmm, not bad," I said. "Grab a roll of thin wire and a pack of eyes." We moved on and found ourselves in plumbing.

"What are we gonna do with stuff like this?" asked Carla. "Build a toilet?"

"I need some PVC pipe, some quick cement, a few couplings..."

"For what?"

"A potato cannon, of course," I said.

"Pota...a what?" she asked.

"It shoots stuff," I explained. "Not just potatoes, but anything you can stuff in the barrel. It's powered by any flammable gas like hairspray, WD40, butane, etc."

"Oh, yeah, pyro stuff. Got it." I chose a coupling, two sizes of pipe, a can of cement and an end cap from the display.

"We have to get an electronic click igniter—like for a barbeque—and some flammable aerosol."

Bart got an idea. “Hey, how about some of this smaller PVC for blowguns?”

“What? Like, *you* know how to make poison darts” I said, shooting down his idea. We beelined to the outdoor aisle and found the barbeque replacement parts section, picking up a sparker unit and an Aim n’ Flame lighter, then went back to hardware for a couple of awls the right size to bore holes in the PVC pipe for a filling valve and the igniter. While in the section I grabbed a cheap hammer, hatchet, pliers, a small wire cutter and screw driver—all but the hatchet came in a kit and they were pink (Carla liked that).

“Flares,” said Carla, “don’t forget flares.” On the way to the small automotive section for road flares, we passed an aisle loaded with things like butane torches, small bottles of propane and canned butane. *A pyros dream aisle.* We picked up a couple of each then rounded out the shopping spree with a couple coils of nylon rope, a bag of shop rags, three flashlights, a twelve pack of flares, a brick of batteries, a twelve by sixteen foot tarp and a five gallon can of paint thinner. We passed on the duct tape. Forty minutes later we checked out to the raised eyebrows of the clerk.

* * *

Two hours later, give or take a few minutes, Bart, Carla and I were on our way from Lowes to Honey Island Swamp armed with a cab trunk full of hardware. I had originally tried to ditch Carla by telling her we would go the hardware store and swing back by for her. But, you know, she's as smart as she is pretty and wouldn't let us out of her sight. Besides, the Lowes was on the way.

The cab driver rolled his eyes at us but asked no questions. I guess cash fare was cash fare. On the way I assembled the potato cannon with the windows rolled down to alleviate the toxic fumes from the plumber's cement.

We arrived at the tour location, paid the driver sixty-bucks, leaving the whole of $9.74 left among us. It was around 12:30 p.m. and all was quiet. It was dark except for a single mercury vapor street light illuminating the dock an eerie green-yellow. A gentle breeze blew in off the water. The *mouche a fea** flitted in the distance. The cab driver pulled up to the dock as we instructed and sat wringing his hands and looking around like he was nervous while we unloaded. Finally we waved him off. I think he was glad to get out of there.

"Bart, pick a boat and see if everything's in order with the outboard. Carla and I will get batteries into these lanterns and get organized. When you're done…oh, don't start anything until we're ready…when you're done come on back and we'll get loaded."

"Sho nuff," he said and took off down the dock. I called Reed and let him know we'd arrived at position A and that we were okay while Carla went rummaging through our collection of plastic bags, pulling out heavy duty flashlights. I soon joined her at the task and found the blister pack of batteries, but couldn't for the life of me get it open.

Carla picked up one of the lanterns and opened the battery chamber. I rummaged again and found the box knife we'd bought. It was in a blister pack. *How are you supposed to get a box knife out of a blister pack without a box knife?*

"I need a knife or something," I whispered. Carla dug into the pocket of her jeans and pulled out a pocket knife. I smiled. *Gotta love a girl who carries a knife—or else*, I mused. I pulled the blade open and tore into the blister packs, handing batteries to Carla who arranged them in the cavities of the lanterns. She tested her work with her hand over the lens and flipped the light back off. We finished that project just as Bart jogged up the dock.

"No gas, no gas tanks," he said, huffing.

"You're kidding me!"

"Nope. Probably take them out of the boats at night so that no one can take off with them."

"Ya think?" I said.

"Ya think to look in the boathouse over there?" said Carla. Man, did I mention she was bright? Bart trotted off toward the boat house and traipsed down the gangplank.

I turned back to Carla, "I'm glad you came along."

"You'd have thought of it," she replied nonchalantly as she removed the two coils of rope from our bags and draped them over her neck and shoulders. I dug into our wares again and removed the hatchet and secured it in my belt. She bent down and fished out a couple of the flares and the pink-handled hammer from the girlie tool kit. She ripped open the package of flares and placed them on the ground, took the hammer and began beating them.

"What are you doing!?" I cried. She stopped and looked up with a smile.

"My brother, Josiah, always did this to his Piccolo Pete's on the Fourth of July. It makes them explosive. Mom, hates it when he does it. Anyway, I figure these will work the same way."

"Wow, great idea, but don't do them all, we might need some for signaling."

"Gotcha." She went back to pummeling flares.

Bart was back, "I need some bolt-cutters; it's locked."

"Don't have any," I said, reaching to my belt. "Here, take this hatchet and chop through the door if you have to."

"Got it." And bam, he was jogging back down the dock again. *Pretty good shape for a chunky guy.* Meanwhile Carla loaded the flares back into the bags, putting the beat up ones in one bag and the unaltered ones in another. *Man, why didn't I think of that idea.* They looked like sticks of dynamite. Now, maybe they would function like them. *What a woman!*

Bart was back again carrying two gas tanks, hatchet in his belt. "They're going to need a new door," he huffed and headed off to the boat. Carla and I gathered up our supplies and followed.

9 OFF AND RUNNING

After hooking up the gas lines to the tanks and pumping the primer Bart gave the outboard's starter cord a yank and the engine sputtered to life with a plume of acrid exhaust. Carla and I stowed the gear on board and sat. Soon we were underway. Bart stood near the stern at the wheel of the boat as he gingerly trolled us out into the watercourse. "You remember the way?" I asked.

"Like duh," Bart replied. "Have you ever known me to get lost?"

"Only in thought," said Carla as Bart gunned the throttle and the chilly air and spray whipped over us. *At least it keeps the mosquitoes away.* We tugged on our jackets. Carla clicked on one of the heavy duty flashlights and aimed it over the bow. The outboard thrummed and whined as the boat cut through the murky water. The light shone eerily ahead, illuminating only a few yards of the waterway forward of the boat. I thought of how sometimes the path of life before us only showed the next few steps and did not light God's whole plan. *Thy word is a lamp unto my feet and a light unto my path** I quoted from the Psalms to myself. What lay ahead, I had no idea. I guess I would know when I got there—maybe. I hoped.

I wasn't particularly keen on bayous at night. The last time we were out in the marshes and swamps we ran into terrorists and zombies, but even without such dangers there were alligators and snakes. Did I mention I hate snakes? Honestly, bayous are creepy places—especially at night. Dark gray tentacles of Spanish moss swayed eerily from the scrubby trees, the moon—a sliver of silver in the brooding sky—gave little illumination, but still carved haunting shadows across the murky water.

The three of us were alone in new territory and people had gone missing. Two of the three were my dad and Bart's dad—trained law enforcement personnel. What were three kids going to do? We too could turn up missing. We could die.

Bart swung our vessel—not ours really—east, down a narrow channel overhung with cypress toward Hap's place. The trees formed an arched canopy that cut out even more moonlight. He throttled back the outboard to maneuver more carefully through the creepy labyrinth. *Labyrinth*, that made me think of David Bowie.* Talk about creepy.

"It's just up ahead," said Bart, yelling above the chug of the engine, "around a couple of bends." I didn't doubt him, but Carla snorted. Bart had a sixth sense about navigation and could remember how to get anywhere he'd ever been before.

"And you know this, how?" she asked.

"Trust him," I said, "he knows." Two turns later, there it stood, leaning like a wounded soldier, proud and brave, but injured none-the-less: Hap's camp, stilted and weathered, silhouetted against the shadowy *bos coya** that surrounded it. Bart smirked at Carla and throttled back some more, easing the boat up to the wharf next to the airboat our dads had borrowed. I jumped up and made my way to the gunnel near the bow, grabbed the tie line and secured it to the dock.

After he cut the engine, Bart did the same in the stern. We sat there in silence, listening for a minute. There was the gentle lapping of the water, the hum of mosquitoes, the croak of frogs, the groaning of the shack and the flap of the police tape in the breeze—nothing out of the ordinary (aside from the police tape, that is).

Out of the blue Bart rattled off, "Did you guys know that the words listen and silent have the same letters only in a different order?"

“Well, that’s interesting, Bart,” I said, picking up a flashlight. “Let’s have a look around.” Side by side Bart and I, followed by Carla, crept out of the boat and gingerly ascended the stairs to the *gallerie**. The three of us stopped in unison outside the door that moaned on its hinges, ajar. No light came from the crack and I pressed my hand against the door, swinging it open with a creak and shining my light inside.

Searching the room with the beam, my sight fell upon the forensic kit sitting on the bed toppled to one side, contents spilling out. Carla’s light joined mine and scanned the room and we stepped further inside after Carla looked behind the door with trepidation. Bart walked over to ‘kitchen’ counter. Roaches scuttled away from the light.

The place was pretty much the same as we had left it only hours before except for the kit and a few more muddy, four-toed footprints—some were scuffed as if something was dragged through them. I knelt down for a closer examination. “They’re still moist and fresh,” I whispered and pointed to one that had been smeared. Bart swung his light around the nearby floor and stopped the beam on another partial print.

“Look here,” he said. “That looks like a boot print.”

“*Fo troo*,” I replied. “See how it’s scuffed across the floor?”

“Uh, huh,” said Bart.

"Probably a scuffle."

"Scuff, scuffle, makes sense," said Carla.

"Not good," intoned Bart, ignoring her smart remark.

"There are others," I said, thinking the prints might have come from our dad's shoes. I stood and scanned the room again. Nothing. I went to the bed.

"Well," said Carla, "we know they were here and we know the monster returned. There may have been a scuffle and now they're not here."

Bart put his hands on his hips and said, "The question then is: Where did they go?"

"It doesn't look like there are any more clues," I said, gathering up the lab-field equipment from the bed and stuffed it back into the kit. Bart turned back to the door and took a step. I heard a tinkling noise from where his foot stepped and shone my light down at his feet and gasped. There on the floor, rolling to a stop, was the spent casing from a police issue Glock*—my dad's sidearm!

Well, it might not actually be police issue and it may or may not be my dad's; it would take a ballistics expert to confirm that. However, the Glock was, after all, the sidearm of choice for sixty-five percent of U.S. law enforcement officers. I bent down and picked it up, looked at it and stuffed it into the pocket of my jeans. Probably not the best crime scene etiquette. I scanned for more casings. There were none.

"Time to move on," instructed Bart. I nodded and we went back outside and did a once-over of the *gallerie* and dock. I took out my phone to report back to Reed. It showed two bars. Reception was dropping off. *Dead zone*, I thought, then wished I hadn't. I dialed and he picked up.

"Hey, Reed," I said.

"Call me Redeye," he said. "That's my…ode name."

"Okay, 'Redeye'," I glanced at the others, rolling my eyes. "This is The Rock." That had just dawned on me since my name meant 'rock' in Hebrew. Besides that's what they use to call Dwayne Johnson, the wrestler, turned movie action figure. *Yeah, that's me: The Rock*. "We're at point B. It's confirmed, our dads have been here. We found the kit and airboat just as was reported. We also found fresh prints and possible signs of a scuffle. Someone fired a round—there was a casing on the floor. Could be Dad's gun; don't know. We're moving on now, but I don't know where."

"You're kind...break…up," he said. "What's tha…you said about..ooting?" *Shooting.*

"Dad, I think, shot his gun. No idea at what. Anyway, I've only got two bars out here. Reception could get worse."

"Two what?"

"Bars."

"Roger tha..." *Roger?*

"Okay, I'll call back if and when I can. Roger that?"

"Ca…back, okay?" said the staticy voice on the other end of the failing connection.

"If I can."

"Yeah."

"Over."

I hung up after returning an *over*. "Let's go."

Back in the boat, Bart gave the starter cord a yank and brought the outboard back online as Carla and I untied the lines. Soon we were back out on the channel heading further east at a slow crawl with Carla aiming a light over the bow.

"We're not going to sneak up on anyone this way," I yelled above the motor.

"Did you want to swim, then?" he asked.

"Didn't bring my Speedo," I said. Carla chuckled. I didn't wear a Speedo, I had trunks. "I'm just sayin'…"

"When I find an interesting place to trawl into, we can get out and do some exploration on foot, okay?"

"Interesting?" inquired Carla.

"He means 'with potential,' like as in something that might be worth looking into."

"Like?"

"I don't know. Lights, other people, a space ship, perhaps." I smirked.

"Ha ha." She shivered from the cold air and spray, so I scooted closer and wrapped my arms around her as Bart ruddered southeast up an even thinner channel. Clusters of duck grass encroached upon the sides of the boat and Bart slowed. I yawned and snuggled in closer to Carla, laying my head on her shoulder.

"We'd best keep our eyes peeled, *padnet*," said Bart. He was right; if we were going to find our fathers I had best be alert. America needs more lerts. They also need round tuits, but that's another joke. I lifted my head and scanned the marshland around us. Patches of earth and piles of downed limbs rose up from the levee—or water's edge—along with the musky smell of decaying vegetation.

In the sunshine these branches would sport many a sunning snake. Being reptiles they are cold-blooded and need to warm themselves in order to raise their body temperature. *I wonder where snakes go in the night?* I shuddered then began to nod off.

* * *

"Pete, Pete," said Bart awaking me. I rubbed the sleep from my eyes.

"Sup?"

"He's found an 'interesting' spot to dock," said Carla.

"Yeah?" I said, looking around. Bart had cut the outboard down to a crawl and was moving toward the bank through a thicket of duck grass and lilies. "What is it?"

"Nothing really," he said, "just Honey Island. At least I think it is. It's an island anyway. I've been around it once now and there's a boat pulled into a lagoon about quarter a mile back."

"You see anyone? Or they see you?"

"No, I didn't. I don't think we were seen, or heard. No signs of a camp. Just a yacht anchored in the lagoon."

"A yacht?"

"Might be a private research vessel, but it looks like a yacht. Maybe a forty-footer and nice as best I could tell."

"That *does* sound interesting. We gonna check it out?"

"That's the plan."

We gathered our gear—plastic sacks full of hardware—as Bart beached the boat. I scuttled out and helped Carla to shore. She looked like a bandito with coils of rope over each shoulder like a pair of bullet sashes. Bart handed us the parcels and jumped out as well. I took out my phone. One bar. Probably couldn't get reception that was decent enough for a call, but a text might get through. I quickly texted Reed…ah, Redeye:

huny isld

found yacht

nothing nown yet

confirm by txt

the rock

Hopefully he'd text back. I'd check later.

10 MARSH MONSTER

We set out on foot along the marshy shore of the island. Not wanting to risk being seen, we didn't use the flashlights. It was easy enough to follow the waterline in pale glow of the crescent moon, but the lack of light did slow us down a bit. Marshland can look quite solid when it isn't, so careful steps are in order. Bart took the lead (carrying the paint thinner) and I in the rear behind Carla, each of us lugging a plastic sack of assorted stuff we hoped would be useful.

"I wish we had backpacks," whispered Carla. "This sack is heavy and it's cutting into my hand. I have to switch hands every few minutes."

"I can carry it for you," I volunteered.

"I can pull my own weight, Pete." *Snippy*

"Oh, I know, I know, but I don't mind, really, helping you." I do *try* to be a good boyfriend.

"I'll be okay. Thanks."

Truth be told, my own sack was cutting into my hand and I had to switch frequently, as well. It wasn't the best of circumstances, but it would have to do. About fifteen minutes later I could see the yacht bobbing offshore and we hunkered down behind a stand of cypress to form our next plan of action.

"Look," I said, "we have no idea what we're walking into. It could be nothing, it could be some serious trouble. Carla, I want you to hang back behind us, out of sight, so in case we're seen and we do run into trouble, you can phone Reed and relay what's happening—hopefully he can be reached...*if* we need to."

"What?"

"You heard me, here's my phone. It's on vibrate. It's safer, and we need a back-up."

"I don't want to become separated..."

"I know, but it's the best plan. Let's stash some gear here." I sat my sack down behind a cypress and the others did the same.

"So, what's the plan, Stan?" asked Bart. "I mean, the Rock."

"We climb aboard the yacht and take a look around, I guess."

"How are we gonna get out there?"

"Oh, yeah," said Carla, "I'm not swimming with gators."

"You're staying behind remember," I said. "And gators aren't out at night, I think."

"You think?" said Bart. "Well, I'm not swimming either."

"Then, I guess we travel inland," I said picking up my sack. "Get your gear."

"I want a code name, too" said Carla. Okay, all my friends were nuts. As they say, 'birds of a feather flock together'.

"Okay, how 'bout Gator Girl?" said Bart.

"How about M?" she asked.

"You know," I said, "she died in the last Bond movie."

"Uh, okay, I'll go with Gator Girl then."

"Bart?" I supposed he wanted a code name, too.

"Call me" he said, thinking, "…uh…the Black Knight."

"You mean the Dark Knight as in Batman?" asked Carla.

"No, I was thinking the knight in *Monty Python and the Holy Grail* who keeps on standing guard as all his appendages are cut off."

"It's only a flesh wound," I quoted.

"That's the one," he said.

"Okay then, Black Knight, Gator Girl, let's go."

Carla took hold of my arm and felt what little muscle I had, "Okay," she said, giggling, "Rock."

"You should see my peck pop," I grinned. "Come on, follow me." I took off toward the boat and turned inland. We crept along slowly and cautiously keeping to what timber we could. After a short time Bart stopped dead in his tracks. "What?" I asked in a whisper.

"My eyes are playing tricks on me, *padnet*. Look!" He gestured with his free arm. "Over there." I nearly wet my pants when I saw what he saw. There in the distance, not twenty yards from us, hunched a greenish-brown figure with glowing green eyes backlit with an eerie blue glow.

"Is that, is that…" I said.

"What you think it is?" Bart nodded. Carla came up to us from the rear. Bart gave her the universal *shhh* sign and, seeing what we saw, she gasped. The slicked down, hairy creature lumbered back and forth like it was guarding a nest. I signaled a retreat and we fell back behind some shrubbery. *Ni!* I thought. After some discussion we decided to circle south and see what we could from the rear, not wishing to encounter the creature outright.

* * *

Ten minutes later, there he was again! *Why had it moved along with us? Could it be another creature?* I was baffled. I gestured we continue to circle and we moved on.

"Is that thing," asked Bart, "heading us off?"

"Beats me," I said, "or maybe there're two of them."

"What's that glow behind them?" asked Carla.

"Search me," answered Bart. "Mother ship?"

"I think we need to get back there," said Carla. "See what they're guarding."

"Yeah," I said, "let's keep moving." And we did. Another ten minutes and there was *another* creature. I was really wondering what was going on. *Was this a secret UFO landing site? Were these really swamp monsters guarding their nursery?*

I noticed the breeze coming at us from the creature's direction, "You smell anything?"

"No, why?" said Bart. "You let one rip?"

"If I did you'd be dead right now," I retaliated. "Aren't these swamp things supposed to smell awful?"

"That's what they say," said Carla.

"Well," I said, "the wind is coming from his direction and I don't smell anything. Do either of you?"

"Not really," said Carla while Bart shook his head.

"Weird," I said. "Anyway, what are we going to do?"

"We're going to have to take one out, if we're going to get past," said Bart. "But we have to do it without alerting the others."

"*Fo troo*," I said. "How we gonna do that?"

"You're the genius," he said.

"Thanks, yeah, leave it to ol' Peter."

"The Rock," interjected Carla.

"Okay, what's in our utility belt, Batman?"

"Black Knight. And you know as well as I do, Rock. Bat gun, bat flares, bat torch, bat…"

"I know, I know, okay? Let me think." I thought. *Well, lessee, there was the ol' Rambo rush—the run and gun. That wouldn't work; too noisy. The Katniss Everdeen hornet nest maneuver from Hunger Games. Probably not, I hate bees. Best thing to do is draw it away from its post and sneak behind. But how? The ol' rock in the brush? Nah. Think, think.* I thought and thought for a good five minutes before I came up with what I hoped was a reasonable plan. Hopefully, this thing was dumb enough to fall for it.

"Okay, I think I have something."

"What movie is it from?" asked Bart.

"Ha ha," I said.

"Well, they've always worked for you before," said Bart.

"I guess this is sort of based on a premise from many a Western, if that helps. You know how the cowboys always stick their hat on a stick and raise it up over a boulder to draw fire?"

"Yeah, but, Dallas ain't here an' we got no hat," said Carla in a southern drawl, putting her thumbs in her waistband and standing bow-legged.

"That's not the point," I said. "What we have to do is draw him out then sneak behind him. We need a diversion, so here's what we're going to do. Bart, I'm going to twist a screw-eye into this tree. I'm going to tie some of this nylon rope to the loop. You are going to do the same thing, screw-eye, tied off line, tight…"

"Taut," corrected Carla, removing the rope from over her shoulder.

"Taut. Tied off to that tree way over there. You see it?"

"Uh huh."

"Carla. Meanwhile you gather some limbs, tree limbs, two legs, two arms. Then I'll wire together a dummy using the tarp for a covering. We rig up a second line and use it like a pulley to which we attach the dummy and pull it across the clearing like its walking. The swamp thing is either going to try to scare it off, attack it, or run off and hide. Understand?"

"No," said Carla.

"It's like a decoy," explained Bart.

"Just gather the limbs, and keep it quiet." I instructed and she set off. I rummaged through our gear and fished out the package of screw-eyes, the tarp and the nylon rope. I tied the end of the cord onto a screw-eye, handed the cord and another eye to Bart along with the pliers. "You might need these to twist the eye into the tree."

"What about you?"

"I'll use the screw driver for leverage. Now go." He hit the dirt and crawled across the open space using the tall grass as cover, letting out the line as he went as I set to work boring the screw-eye into the tree beside me. The creature continued to pace back and forth in the distance. After a minute or so I was done with the screw eye task and I emptied the bag of rags into one of our sacks and began gathering moss, stuffing it into the bag. That would be the dummy's head.

Carla arrived back with four gnarled sticks—two about six inches around and four feet long, and two about three inches around and three feet long. I took out the wire cutters and wire and fastened the bunch together into a really thin-looking scarecrow, attached the head at the top, running the wire through it and making a loop. Carla and I gingerly opened the tarp and shaped it like a hood around the figure.

"Knife," I whispered, and she pulled it from the pocket of her jeans, handing it to me. Bart returned, crawling across the ground. When he stood up, his front was covered with mud. I cut the tarp up the middle from the bottom to the top and across each side about a foot underneath each of the 'arms' and cut pieces of cord to tie them to the sticks, thus forming sleeves and pant legs, and tied a cord below the head to form a neck. *Blue Man**, I thought. "Ready for another trip, Bart?"

"Sure," he answered, "I need some more mud." I attached the dummy decoy to the remainder of the line and handed an end to Bart.

"Here, this one goes through the screw-eye, but don't tie it off, bring the end back. And take this other coil of rope in case you need to tie it to the other to make it longer."

"Will do," he said, lying back down on the ground. While he was gone I wired a flashlight onto the dummy's arm while Carla loaded the trash and supplies back into the sacks. Five minutes or so later Bart came crawling back and handed me the second line.

"I had to tie them together," he said. "What now?"

"You guys go on ahead in that direction," I indicated to my right, the dummy on our left. "I'll switch on the dummy's flashlight and follow you, pulling the line. The dummy should move across the open space. We'll see what happens. If the creature moves out toward the dummy, start circling in toward that eerie light. I'll meet up with you in a few." They nodded and set off. I counted to one hundred before switching on the dummy light, crouched low and took off after them, looking back over my shoulder.

The dummy lurched along the line with a slight bobbing motion in sync with each of my steps in the opposite direction. Immediately I—or rather the dummy—had the creature's attention. It stopped in its tracks and observed for a moment before rushing to a nearby stump and picking up what looked like a rifle. *Ha! Human*, I thought to myself, *Knew it*. Now it was bounding through the brush toward the decoy. *Perfect. I'm a genius.*

Behind me I heard the words, "Hold it right there, buddy." The male voice was too far back from me to be addressed at me so I kept on. The 'monster' was talking to the dummy. *Dummy.* I didn't bother looking back; I was running out of line and just then there was a snag—the line wouldn't pull. I yanked and looked back. The dummy was bobbing against a tree. Time to hightail it out of there. I dropped the line and set off in a duck walk, knees burning with the effort.

I found the others with some searching, all the while noting the movements of the man dressed like a yeti. He examined the apparatus and ran back to his stump where he brought something up to his mouth. We were too far away to hear, but I was pretty sure he was using a radio to make a perimeter breach report.

"Follow the light," I said, "*vite, vite**."

* * *

Minutes later we stealthily approached the blue glow, which grew brighter as we drew closer. The chugging sound of generators grew louder, too. It was soon clear that the lights did *not* come from a space ship or some netherworld nursery, but were, in fact, an array of halogen flood lamps illuminating a dig—an archeological research site, perhaps? *But why the sentry of costumed goons then?* We approached with caution staying hidden in the overgrowth and came to another low-lying clump of duck grass where we stopped to observe and converse.

There was a small backhoe at work removing mud from a hole already the size of a backyard shed in volume and depth. A pump exhumed water from the hole, expelling it into a ditch some yards away. Nearby was erected a rather elaborate tent and a man, dressed in dungarees and hip boots, bustled about the area.

"What do you make of that?" I asked the others.

"An excavation?" asked Bart in return, shrugging his shoulders. Carla just shrugged.

"Let's think about this," I said, "Speculations?"

"Exhuming a body?" said Carla.

“Gas or oil mining?” said Bart. That was a big operation down in Louisiana. *Too big and too small*, I thought then gestured for more ideas.

“Treasure hunting?” suggested Bart. “Ah, building…?”

“That’s it!” I exclaimed in hushed tones. “They—whoever they are—are looking for pirate treasure!”

11 PIRATES!

"We have to get down there!" I said.

"You're kidding me," said Carla. "They're…"

"But its treasure," said Bart.

"And they're probably just as violent as Black-beard," Carla finished.

"Maybe," I said. "So we don't get caught. We go in for a looksee and then get out. Okay?"

Pirates? I'd never met a real pirate. It's said that pirates frequented the waters of the lower Mississippi back in the seventeenth to nineteenth centuries. Among them was the infamous buccaneer Jean Lafitte who bartered with the Americans for pardon in exchange for information regarding the attacks of the British Navy. He even fought alongside the states during The War of 1812* and helped win the war in 1815. He was never heard from again, though it is thought that he survived, married and settled in the Bahamas to raise a family. He and his brother had operated a smuggling outfit out of a warehouse down at English Turn (less than forty-five miles from where we sat).

Many have speculated that he buried treasure in these parts and many have looked for it to no avail. *Probably a myth like the swamp monster.* But that didn't keep people from looking. That *had* to be it, it was the perfect site—navigable by the surrounding lakes and rivers; an easy route from one to the other—especially back then.

"Okay," said Carla, "let's say that's it. So why the disguised swamp thugs?"

"Duh," said Bart. "Secrecy, to scare people away."

"But people search for treasure in these parts all the time," said Carla. "No one thinks anything about it."

"Unless…" I interjected with finger in the air, "they were sure they had a good find. You'd protect that."

"Yeah, yeah!" said Bart way too loudly in his excitement.

Shhh! scolded Carla.

"Sorry."

"And," I continued, "if anyone got too close…" I drew my finger across my throat in a slicing motion.

Bart swallowed hard, "Oh no," he said.

I was thinking the same. *Our dads!* It was at that point that one of the costumed swamp goons, minus the head portion (meaning no mask to hide the quite human head), emerged from the tent and began shouting and gesturing 'come on.' That's when the other men dropped what they were doing and went into the tent.

"Uh oh," said Carla. "I think I know what that might mean."

"And I think you're right," I said. "They're on to us."

"And they're going to come looking for us," added Bart.

"Yup," I said as the small army emerged from the canvas shelter toting weapons and scattered in pairs in various directions. "Time to fall back, team."

"Wait," said Bart, "isn't that…isn't…?"

"It's Thachne!" exclaimed Carla quietly.

"No," I said raising my eyebrows, my voice evident with disbelief.

"It *is*," said Bart. My mind raced, trying to piece this puzzle together. We not only needed a plan, but we needed to get away and then we needed to get back into this 'dig' and find out what was going on, find out where our fathers were, hopefully rescue them, and then get off the island and back home. *Could they be in the tent?* Yeah, that's what I was thinking: *Piece of cake, sure.*

"Hold on a moment," I said, pulling out my phone, keeping it low and shrouded in my jacket. I checked for reception. Only one bar and no text from Reed. I knew that a person couldn't text a 911 call and calling them was not an option without better reception. I noted the time, 3:14 in the morning, and cautiously closed the device, slipped it back into my pocket and looked at the others who were looking back at me, hope written on their faces. "Nothing," I said. "We're on our own." I then reiterated our entire situation and my thoughts to Bart and Carla as they silently listened.

"I agree," said Bart, when I'd finished. "We *do* need to explore the camp, or, um, dig, but we have to do it when the opportunity presents itself and that isn't now. It's too dangerous. We need fall back and wait for things to cool down."

"I couldn't agree more," I said softly. "Hide the gear; cover it up," I added. "Especially that paint thinner—hide it good." We went about doing just that. The big things went behind a log and we covered them up with grass and moss. The other items were nestled in their sacks and snuggled down into tufts of duck grass before we came back together. Although we were never far from one another at any point.

"Remember where this is," I said quietly when our heads where so close together I could smell the hints of pizza on the others breaths. "Make mental notes of our position." My stomach rumbled—it had been hours since we ate. *Or was it just nerves?* I could hear rustling in the brush off to our right. "Come on, quietly." I turned left in my squatting position and went prone in the muck, crawling with my elbows, as the others followed suit.

* * *

Now we were all well caked in an icky-smelling swamp grime, but no one complained. We were, after all, alive and free. There's something to be said about that, don't you think? Yeah, life can be scary, perilous, a pain and full of hardships, but it also has its simple joys. *Thank you Jesus*, I prayed, *keep our dads safe—and Hap, too*. Had I not even thought to pray for them until now? I'm afraid I'm not the Christian I often think I am. I would have to work on that.

I led our group back toward the island's shore and toward our boat, making sure to keep to the cover of vegetation. When we arrived, it was just as I'd feared: Our vessel had been discovered and was now guarded by one of the goons—this one not costumed as a marsh monster. I stopped in my vantage point not twenty yards from where he stood and motioned Bart and Carla up beside me. "You see that?" I whispered.

"I do," said Bart. "Not good."

"Expected though," I commented.

"What are we going to do?" asked Carla. "How are we going to get off the island?"

“We’ll find a way,” Bart assured, “but we have other matters to consider first.” We were running out of time. It was now close to four in the morning and the sun would be cracking over the horizon in another hour and a half—give or take. We had to get a plan in motion.

“Nothing we can do here,” I said. “Back the way we came. Let’s see if our stuff is safe and see if we can come up with a plan. We’ll have about an hour to do it, whatever it is. Sun’ll be up before long.”

12 ENDANGERED SPECIES

We made our way through the marsh back to our stash and found it undisturbed. The night was alive with the sound of music—the music of the night. *Cool. Two stage musical references in one thought.* But the music was all pretty creepy-like. Frogs croaked, mosquitoes buzzed, owls hooted, wild boar snorted and gators groaned in the shadows. It was enough to set ones nerves on edge. Running into the tusk of a hunting pig or into the jaws of a hungry gator was not something I wanted to do.

At one time alligators were an endangered species, but they have come back and, though heavily regulated, the hunting of gator is once again allowed. They were endangered because they were hunted and killed relentlessly for the hide (and the meat's pretty tasty, too). That's how I felt—hunted for my skin and meat. If we were caught *we* would be endangered. Maybe even 'extinct,' if you get my drift.

Down here, in southern Louisiana, the land is flat as a pancake; there are no mountains, there are no caves. The best one can do for cover is find a low place behind some foliage and hunker down…and hope, you aren't found. And, quite frankly, you didn't just want to climb into any old hidey-hole for fear of gators and spiders and, heaven forbid, snakes. Plus there were cougars and bears and all manner of other natural threats. But, that's what we had to do.

With as much stealth as possible we searched for someplace to take cover near where we'd left our goods. Fortunate for us each pair of goons made plenty of noise traveling through the brush and we were able to avoid them, though their activity had died down considerable and backhoe man was back to work as was pump guy.

At last we found our stash, gathered it up and located a reasonable place to hide. It was low and tangled with vines, twisted with gnarls of dead wood and laden with tall fern. However, it was quite damp. We lay there on our backs, huddled together behind the pile of woodland debris and spoke in soft tones. The stars were out (as were the mosquitoes), showing through a thin canopy of trees against an ever lightening sky. We'd seen it go from near black to dark purple.

"You know," said Carla, "I prefer to sleep in my bed."

"Well," I said, "we won't be doing any sleeping tonight."

"You know what I mean," she responded.

"Sure, now what are we going to do?"

"I have no idea," said Bart. "I'm just the brawn; you're the brains."

"Oi! And what am I?" asked Carla. "Chopped liver?"

"No, but, no offense, you smell like it," I said.

"It's called *parfum' de swamp*," she retorted. "You like?"

"Where did that expression, 'like chopped liver,' come from?" asked Bart.

"I believe it was a Jewish or Yiddish* phrase used to express exasperation," said Carla. "Meaning 'I never get the lime-light' because liver was, like a side dish. Now who's the brains?"

"Yeah," I said, "we're all going to be chopped liver, if we can't figure out how to get out of this—and soon. We *have* to see what's in that tent and what's in that pit."

"And?" asked Bart.

"And I think I have a plan," I said. Carla sighed and I spoke quickly. "Indiana Jones did it in *Raiders of the Lost Ark*, though it's not original in the movie, Bond's done it, too, but I digress, the point is we sneak up on a guard, incapacitate them, and steal their outfit in order to infiltrate the nest." I took a breath and finished my thought, "We need a swamp monster costume."

"Those dudes are toting guns," reminded Bart.

"I am aware of that," I said. "Stealth is in order, okay."

"So, why do I get the sinking feeling, that *I* am the stealth?" asked Bart.

"Because you are," I said.

"What am I going to do? Bonk one of them on the back of the head with a rock? What if I kill it, uh, him? I don't want that on my conscience. What makes you think…?"

"Stop rattling," said Carla. "Use your Vulcan nerve pinch, Tuvak*."

"Just because I'm black doesn't make me Tuvak…"

"I was talking about the pointy ears."

"Why not Spock then?"

"You got me there."

"Okay, you two," I said, "quit bickering. Listen, the plumber's cement we bought, its ether based. You just have to swab it out on one of the rags and hold it over his nose."

"What if it sticks to his face?" asked Bart. "And what makes you think I can get that close and overpower him? They've got AK-47s, dude!"

"Look, you've got twenty pounds on me, Bart. Besides you're part Houma Indian, You've got more sneak."

"You guys are *so* racist," he said with a smirk. "Let the minority do the dirty work. Okay, but only because you're such a wimp."

"I knew you'd understand," I said pulling the container of plumber's cement from the bag while Carla got a rag. "Now get cracking, *padnet*." Bart took the items and traipsed off. I took out my phone and checked for a text from Reed. No such luck and still only one bar.

I sent Reed another text, with our location and situation asking him to send in help, hoping it would go through. Texts have a way of getting through even with lower reception when calls won't, though sometimes it takes time. I would endeavor to send one every half hour.

I was worried. Sure Bart was strong, but goons where dangerous—trained in the martial arts and stuff. *Right?* That was probably more movie theatrics than real life. I thought back to our visit to CIA headquarters. We'd seen their training facilities and program. *Did Thanche have a training program? Did he hire professionals?* I regretted that I'd sent Bart on this mission. He was my friend; *I* should have gone. *Was this even going to work?*

13 TAKE DOWN

In the distance we watched as Bart crept up behind one of the goons. He went slowly and undetected. At last he crouched into position, ready to spring, and waited for the guy to make his pass back in front of him. Timing and stealth would be everything. "You think he can pull it off?" whispered Carla.

"Hey, it's Bart we're talking about. Sure." But I wasn't all that sure myself. We watched and waited while the man turned and started back across his post drawing closer to where Bart lay in wait. Just a few steps more and it should happen. I readied myself to run in with assistance should it be needed. Exactly how I might be able to help, I didn't know.

And then it happened: Bart sprang from the brush and threw his massive arms around the goon. One arm went all the way over the man's throat. Bart's other hand held the rag and he smashed it against the goon's nose and mouth, holding it there with all he was worth as the goon thrashed about wildly. Bart wrapped his legs around the man and they fell to the ground.

A minute later the thrashing stopped and they lay there entangled on the earth. I rose from my crouched position and made a dead run as best I could through the brush toward the pair, with Carla on my heels. Bart was just crawling out from under the subdued guard when we arrived.

“I did it!” Bart exclaimed quietly panting for air, “I did it!”

I bent down and removed of the hood and shirt of the monster costume. I noticed several empty cans of energy drink lying in the mud. *The goon must have been trying to stay awake on his post.* “You sure did, buddy,” I said, working quickly. “I knew you would. Can you give me a hand?” Bart went to work on the guy’s pants and foot coverings. Carla pulled off his webbed gloves.

“Here,” said Carla, handing Bart a rag and what was left of our rope, “bind and gag.”

“Looks like this is going to fit me best,” I said, examining the footwear that was something akin to a green-brown knee-high stocking with a hard four-toed sole attached. “Ingenious.”

“Well, put it on,” said Carla, handing me the gloves and pants. I laid them next to me on top of a nearby stump and, after taking off my jacket, pulled the costume shirt over my head.

“Pants next,” I said. “You might want to turn away if you don’t want to see my boxers.”

“They’re Sponge Bob Square Pants,” teased Bart. (Truth be told they were *Iron Man* boxers. Okay?) Carla turned away without comment and I slipped out of my shoes and jeans then pulled on the monster trousers. I put my own clothes into one of the sacks. Soon I had on the footwear and gloves.

“Aren’t you kinda short for a stormtrooper?” asked Carla when she’d turned around. *Haha.* She was starting to pick up my movie quoting vibe. Bart laughed.

“Laugh it up fuzz-ball,” I said with a Han Solo smirk. “Now, here’s the plan. I’m going to walk into the camp like I belong and walk directly into the tent to see if our dads are in there. Things could go one of three ways: One, Thachne will be in there and I’ll have to have an excuse for the interruption to get me back out. Two, Thachne won’t be in there and it will be a piece of cake. Or three, someone will question me, find out I’m not one of them and I’ll be captured.”

“Take the AK-47,” said Carla. “That will serve as a deterrent.”

“I am *not* shooting any one,” I said.

"I didn't say you would. It's just a prop. The guard would have it on him and you can threaten with it, if need be." Bart handed me the semi-automatic weapon.

"Makes sense, but the thought chills me."

"Think of it like an acting gig," said Bart. "Improvise." *I could do that.*

"Okay, here goes." I started off, but Carla caught my arm and pulled me into an embrace, planting a kiss on my mouth.

"Good luck," she said. I set off feeling energized.

* * *

I hurried into the camp with as much bravado as I could muster, holding the AK-47 across my chest. *Hope I look confident.* No one took a second look as I approached the tent. *Here goes.* Pulling aside the flap, I ducked inside. Nervous sweat dripped down the inside of my costume. There was a Persian rug on top of a tarp floor, the room apportioned like those to which nomadic sheiks might be accustomed, only more modern. The spicy scent of bayberry drifted from an incense burner which sat upon a table at which Thachne worked—a set of books and charts before him. He looked up from his work. "Yes?" *Come on Peter, think!*

"Sir," I began in my deepest voice, still thinking on my feet and trying to find my 'motivation' (that's an actor's term), "there's a perimeter breach. Intruder alert." I noted that no one else was in the room. *No dads here.*

"What happen to 'hey, boss'? Perimeter breach? What kind of talk is that? Who are you?" *Uh, oh. Cover blown. Run!* I turned and ran from the tent. I kept running. Thachne came out after me yelling, "Stop that man!" I ran for all I was worth, veering away from my friends, though close enough to yell to them my last bit of direction before angling away.

"Run. Hide, Split up. Leave the gear." They immediately ran in the opposite direction as the pit workers dropped what they were doing and came after us in pursuit. Fortunately, in their single-minded effort to catch us, the pursuing men didn't pass near our stash. Shots rang out behind me and I leapt over a log and hit the dirt face first. Or, as it were, hit the mud face first, skidding to a stop in the muck and mire. When I rolled over I was greeted by the sight of two AK-47 barrels pointed at my face.

14 OF MONSTERS AND MEN

I was bound, and tossed like a fresh catch of shrimp, into the hold of the yacht. Flailing down the stairs, I heard the hatch door lock behind me as I fell into a heap on the floor, moaning in pain as my ribcage hit the bottom step with a dull thud. *Great! Now what?*

"Welcome to paradise," said a voice in the dark. "What you in for?" *Wait, I know that voice!*

"Who said that?" I asked.

"Pete, Pete, is that *you*?" This second voice I certainly knew; it was my dad.

"Dad!" I cried, dragging myself toward the voice.

"Peter! What are you doing here?"

"Do you have to ask?"

"Came to rescue the old man, huh? You shouldn't have, you know that."

“Is Bart with you?” asked the other man whom I now knew was Bart’s dad.

“Yes, and no,” I answered. “He came out with me, but I think he got away with Carla.”

“You brought Carla on this?!” Dad’s voice was emphatic, even angry.

“She insisted, I tried to…”

“You just don’t know when to… Peter Jackson Myers! For crying out loud! This is dangerous!” He used my full name and we all know what that means.

“I can tell.” *Oops.*

“Don’t be smart with me, young man,” he said curtly.

“Sorry, Dad, but you know I *had* to,” I said sheepishly, pulling myself to a sitting position.

“You don’t *have* to do anything; you *choose* to. And I don’t know what’s with you, Peter.”

“I guess he takes after the old man,” said Warden Davis.

“You keep ou…” began Dad, but halted. “I, I guess you’re right. Peter, I’m sorry. I know you mean well. It’s just that…”

“I know, Dad. I’m just glad you’re alive.”

“I suppose you have a plan…,” he stated, “had a plan.”

“I did, sort of.” Bart’s dad coughed in the dark. “And Warden Davis, I’m sure that Bart and Carla are okay.”

“Let’s hope so,” he said. “So, tell us what’s going on. I’m sure you’ve found out something.”

“As a matter of fact, I *do* know a little. Did you see the hole they’re digging?”

“What hole?” asked Dad. “All we know is that Dr. Thachne is up to something and that he has a fake Swamp Monster out here.”

“Not *a* fake monster,” I said, “an army of them. He’s using them to keep people away.”

“From what?” asked Warden Davis.

“I don’t know, except that he’s excavating something. We think he might be treasure hunting.” My father, or maybe it was Warden Davis, *hmmmed*. My eyes were adjusting to the gloom now; that plus the thin glow of morning light now creeping in from a portal over our heads aided my sight ever so slightly. I couldn’t make out much, but I could tell we were being held in the ship’s galley*. A small door led from the room—*probably to the sleeping quarters or berths as they are called*. “How long have you been here?” I asked, not having much else to say.

“We were captured at Hal’s camp,” said Dad, “sometime before eleven, I’d say. We’ve been in here since—roughly six or seven hours—I would guess, now that the sun’s coming up.”

“Haven’t had a wink of shuteye,” said Warden Davis.

“Have they come back to check on you, give you a bathroom break or anything?”

“That would be no,” answered Warden Davis. “We’d hoped that was what was happening when they threw you in here.”

“And I could use a restroom,” said my dad.

“You could pee in their sink,” I suggested.

“Can’t get up,” he said.

“Tied to something, then?”

“Yes, son, plus they broke my leg.”

“Oh, Dad! No!” I said, clambering over to him in the growing light.

“It’s okay, Pete,” he said. “It’s not a compound fracture.”

I am not one prone to swear, but an inglorious name came to mind. *Let no unwholesome thing come from your mouth**, said the scriptures, which also came to mind, so I bit my tongue. “Warden Davis, are *you* okay?

“I’m a tad hungry,” he answered, “but otherwise I’m fit as a fiddle. I don’t think they meant to harm your father. They would have killed us if they meant harm. They’re just a little rough.”

“A little!?” I was furious.

“What about Hap Deveaux?” asked Bart’s dad. “Have you seen him?”

"No," I answered. "None of us knows what he looks like, but we haven't seen any other prisoners either."

"Uh, Peter," said my dad, "can I ask you a question?"

"Sure, Dad."

"What's with the Halloween costume?"

"Oh, ah, this little thing? I was auditioning for a position on the goon squad."

"Peter?" Dad said, drawing it out.

"Bart knocked out one of Thachne's men, and I traipsed into his camp…"

"A disguise?"

"It didn't work," I said.

"I'd say it works rather well," Bart's dad mused. "Sort of slimming."

"You think so?"

"A little blue boa to offset the eyes and, well…" Bart's dad laughed instead of finishing his sentence.

"Yeah, well, we have to get out of here," I said. "What are our assets?"

"What do you mean?" asked Dad. "They took our guns and radios, we're tied up and I can't really walk all that well."

"These things I know," I said, looking around the room which was growing lighter by the minute. "We're in the galley. There might be knives in a drawer or cupboard—at least some food."

"Did you miss the 'we're tied up' part?" Warden Davis was just like his son (or vice versa). I struggled to get my feet under me and stood—which was difficult with my hands and feet bound—hopped over to the counter and peered in the sink. Nothing there. I scanned the counter. Again, nothing. I turned around, facing away from the counter and tried with my roped hands to pull open a drawer, but it wouldn't budge.

"Try lifting up," suggested Bart's dad. "They're like those in a travel trailer, with a lip." I was about to do that when I heard footfalls on the deck above. Quickly, I crumpled to the floor and slid my body away as quietly as I could. The hatch flew open and in crashed Bart and Carla. Behind them, silhouetted by the rising sun, stood other figures. Two of them parted, leaving a third outlined in shadow.

"Are there any more river rats I should know about?" It was Thachne. After hearing that…that…crook drone on about marsh monsters, I'd know the voice anywhere. I knew something else, too: Bart was about to mouth off.

"I wouldn't tell you if there was and I'm not saying there isn't." *Sure enough.*

"Well, they're going to have to be a lot more clever than the lot of you."

"Bart, don't say anything," reprimanded his father.

"Oh, I'll get what I want out of you," threatened Thachne. "My little operation is too precious to have anything go wrong. But I don't really have the time just now to converse."

"And what operation would that be?" asked my dad.

"Wouldn't you like to know?"

"Actually, I would."

"Well, I'm not telling you, mister policeman. And when I figure out what to do with you…hmm, perhaps a mysterious drowning, a gator feast? Anyway, you won't be around to report anything. Until then, I must get back to my little project. *Adieu**." He turned to go. "Tie them up!" he said to the goons with him and they came down the steps and commenced binding my friends.

"Wait, wait," I yelled up the steps after Thachne. "My father needs medical assistance and we need to use a restroom."

"Good luck with that," he laughed maniacally and disappeared as the two thugs continued tying up my friends. Finally they left, the door slammed shut and the lock was secured. The footfalls fell away and the boat stopped swaying.

"Carla, Bart, are you okay?" I asked.

"Nice of you to ask," said Carla. "A few bumps and bruises and I'm covered in mud, but other than that…"

"I'm fine," added Bart.

"So what happened?" I said wanting to know what they'd accomplished and how they'd been captured.

"You know," said Carla, "running, being captured, tied up, thrown in the cooler. Ever had that happen to you?" (As a matter of fact I had.)

"Been there, done that," said Bart.

"Did you get behind enemy lines, first?"

"No," said Bart. "We were hunted like wild dogs."

"How about our stash?" I asked.

"What stash?" asked my dad, in a way that said he was afraid to ask.

"Just a few things," I answered.

"Like what? Don't say explosives?"

"Might be," I stammered.

"Peter Jackson Meyers" There he went again with the full name.

"Just some flares and paint thinner."

"And a potato cannon," interjected Bart.

"A potato cannon?" questioned Warden Davis, "What were you planning to do with that?"

"Haven't actually decided that," I said. "Carla, do have your knife?"

"No, they took it from me."

"Drat! Okay, back to the drawer," I sighed, struggling again to my feet. And then an anger welled up in me as I thought about those thugs searching my girl. "Did they…did they…"

"No, they didn't touch me," she said, "just had me empty my pockets." I breathed out a sigh of relief, but I was still hopping mad as I hopped over to the drawers. At last I worked one open—lifting up as was suggested. I then turned around and looked inside.

"See anything?" asked my dad.

"Lessee, butter knives, forks, spoons…nope, nothing useful." I hopped sideways, spinning back around in the process, to another drawer, opened it, spun again and peered within. "Can opener, large spoons, spatula…"

"Cool it with the running commentary," chided Bart. "Just find something useful, like a knife."

"So what if we get a knife?" said Carla. "So we get out of our bonds, that door up there, it's solid steel and locked tight."

"Look for a blow torch," said Bart. I rolled my eyes and moved to the third and final drawer. It was what is commonly called a junk drawer and contained nothing but a flashlight, batteries, a roll of string, a hammer, a box of toothpicks…but there I go again with a running commentary. *Wait! What's that?* I turned away from the drawer and rummaged through it, tossing assorted items on the floor until I felt what I was looking for. There it was, in my hand: a pair of wire-cutters.

15 THROUGH THE LOOKING GLASS

Half hour later we had managed to chomp through each other's bonds with the wire cutting tool. By the time we were done my hand was cramped and so was my brain. We hadn't yet settled on how we might escape from our floating prison. We tossed out ideas, ate what food we found and used the restroom. Yeah, we found out that the little door off the galley led down a hallway. The hall also led to another locked steel door at the other end. It had berths along its length and, *thank the Lord*, a bathroom.

A lot to accomplish in a half hour, yes, but we were desperate in more ways than one. Now, we just sat there. I got up to pace the floor. I think better on my feet. It was then that the light hit me. It was the shaft of light beaming in from the portal, but it also gave me an idea. "We can crawl out the window!" I exclaimed.

"I don't think so," said Bart's dad. "It's too small." I walked over and eyed the opening.

"I might be able to do it," I said pulling on the release handle. The window unsealed with the sucking sound of rubber and I climbed atop the dining table to gaze out, squinting in the low sun. I pulled my head back in. "Other than being over water, this should be as easy as pie."

Carla piped in with, "I've had your pie; it ain't that good."

"What are you going to do, if you can get out?" asked Bart.

"I'll go for the blow torch and come back to cut you out."

"You've got a blow torch?" my dad asked, raising his eyebrows.

"Sure," I said, "doesn't everyone?"

"That is if they haven't found our stuff," added Carla.

"You actually have an acetylene cutting torch?" asked Bart's dad.

"No a blow torch and paint thinner," said Bart.

"That's probably not going to work," said Bart's dad. "Doesn't burn hot enough."

"Oh," was all I could muster.

"What else might you have?" asked my father. I reeled through our list of articles, thinking as I did about how one of them might solve our problem. Little came to mind.

"What kind of lock is on the door?" I asked of Bart and Carla who'd seen it in the light.

"A small padlock," said Carla.

"Probably quarter inch thick hasp," added Bart. "Our best bet is probably the hatchet. Maybe."

"Maybe, I can get the hinges off with the screw driver," I said.

"Sounds like a plan," said my dad, "*if* you can get through the window, *if* you get to your stash and *if* you get back here without being caught. That's a lot of ifs and I don't like it."

"We don't have a better plan," I said. "I *have* to try."

"I know you do, son."

"Well then," I said, climbing once again to the portal, "here I go." I stuck my arms out the round little window and pulled myself up, twisting and turning m shoulders, trying to get one through.

"Or not," said Bart. I dropped back from the window, panting.

"Help me up," I said. "I'll try feet first."

"I don't think it will work," said Carla. "Let *me* try."

"No way," I said. "I'm not letting…"

"There you go, pampering me again," she said. "I am perfectly able…"

“I know, I know,” I said. “I’m sorry, but let me try again first.” Bart and his dad hoisted me up and I slid my feet out the opening and wriggled while they shoved, but my hips just wouldn’t go through and they pulled me back inside. I was drenched in sweat. “Okay then…”

“I don’t think it’s a good idea for Carla…” began my dad.

“Mr. Meyers,” Carla cut him off, “with all due respect, I have already saved these boy’s bacon thrice. I can do it again.”

“Saved our bacon!?” I said.

“My knife to open the blister-packs, the idea to…”

“Okay, okay,” I relented.

“I like bacon,” said Bart. We all looked at him for a moment. *Looks like it*, I thought, but kept my mouth shut.

“Let’s do this,” said Carla. Bart’s dad shrugged his shoulders and hoisted her up to the window feet first. Her hips passed through with some effort, but they did. She got hung up at her chest for a moment, but then let out her breath and wriggled through one side at a time. Now she was dangling out the window, Bart and his dad holding her forearms that were bent at the elbows. I stuck my head out between their arms and looked at her hanging over the water.

“Hey, Gator Girl,” I called down, “watch out for alligators.” Her eyes went wide and she glanced around, frantically. She looked back at me with fury on her face.

“Let go,” she called back up. Her arms disappeared through the opening and a second later she splashed down. I poked my head out and saw her thrashing madly for the shore. All of a sudden I felt really queasy and worried. I watched her scramble onto the bank, glad there were no gators around. She turned back and waved, then slogged off into the brush. I pulled my head back inside.

“Brave girl you’ve got there,” said my dad.

“Looks like a keeper,” added Bart’s dad with a wink. Dad gave him a semi-shocked look and Bart’s dad responded to it: “What?”

“You’re right, it won’t be long before he’s hitched,” sighed Dad. I blushed and ran to the toilet to throw up. I told you I was feeling queasy.

16 ARMED AND DANGEROUS

We spent some time looking about the space for weaponry. Wisely the bad guys didn't leave any official ones lying around. We did, however, come up with the following: a fire extinguisher, a box of shotgun shells, sheets off the berths, some olive oil and…get this…a sack of potatoes. I now had a plan and we went to work. When our plan was ready we sat down to further ponder our 'sitch' and worry about Carla.

* * *

Oh, by the way, I also found a cribbage* board and a deck of cards in the cubby over the table and, now as prepared for conflict as we could be, given our assets, we set about playing pairs to pass the time. I was starting to worry. I mean, worry more.

Dad and I were lagging behind, and with the Davis team nearing the finish line, a skunk looked quite possible, though it was now their deal and we would count first. "I'll play through, *padnet*; it ain't over until the fat lady sings."

* * *

We were sunk. Warden Davis had a pair of tens that put them over the line.

"UGH!" *One measly point!* So close to victory, but there were more important matters at hand, we heard footsteps on the deck above! And we froze.

17 CARLA TO THE RESCUE

The rustling of the lock put my nerves on edge. Instantly we were on our feet, cards scattering across the table as we quietly went to our posts and gathered our equipment. Dad poured the olive oil on the steps where we'd removed the non-skid marine carpet. Warden Davis picked up a sheet and stood on one side of the hatch; Bart did the same at the other side. I had my trusty fire extinguisher at the ready.

The shotgun shells, with the shot removed, but the powder left intact and stuffed with toilet paper, had been screwed into the light sockets ready for the throw of the switch manned by my father. (That was something I'd seen in the James Bond film *Skyfall*, albeit a modification—they'd use shrapnel in baggies.) The sack of potatoes? Well, that lay in the corner as we lay in wait. After a moment the fumbling at the lock stopped.

Tang, tang, tang. Metal against metal. My heart leapt inside my chest. *Was that Carla?* Again, *tang, tang, tang.* Bart grabbed a spoon and tapped back. The tapping was returned from the other side. *It had to be Carla.* We all relaxed, but stayed at our posts, quietly listening to a sound—ever so faint—that must have been the work of a screwdriver at the hinges of the small door. I glanced at the clock on the wall: half past nine. It had taken Carla more than an hour to get back. I watched the clock tick around its face as the work continued from the other side. Ten minutes, twelve, fifteen.

"What's taking her so long?" I said. "She should have those screws loose by now."

"You're the only one I know who's got a screw loose," said Bart. *Haha.*

"Peter, I doubt she's adept with a screwdriver," said my dad. "Give her some time. It's not likely an easy task."

"You might be surprised," I said, "Carla's pretty handy." Seventeen minutes later the tapping began again.

"Now what?" said Bart.

"Probably time to knock the door down," suggested Warden Davis, "and hope she's standing aside."

Bart pounded the door twice with his fist and yelled in his loudest voice: "STAND BACK!" His dad laid the sheets down on the slippery steps and Bart took a step back himself and barreled into the hatch. BOOM! The door shook and a crack appeared on the seam to the left. He stepped back and threw himself once again at the door. BOOM! The sound echoed across the swamp and I thought how it carried and how it would probably be heard by Thachne and his goons. The gap widened and Bart rubbed his shoulder. He readied for another run, but his father pushed him aside.

"My turn," he said and took a run at the hatch. BOOM! The door flew open to the right.

"I loosened that for you," said Bart. We scrambled up the steps, Warden Davis first, pushing the door aside.

"Good to see you," said the warden from on deck. Bart and I helped my dad up the steps. At the top I grabbed Carla and gave her a bear hug, but she barely hugged back. She was pale and sweaty. *Probably over exertion in the hot sun.*

"So, what's going on out there?" asked Dad, always the cop.

"They're busy…in the dig," she answered with a ragged cadence of speech, "but not…not with the…heavy equipment. They're down in…in the hole with shovels and picks. I…I climbed a tree so I could see…" She swayed and caught herself on my arm and I took hold of her. She was cold and clammy.

"What's wrong?" asked Bart's dad.

“Snake…”she said, “Snake bite.”

“Oh, no,” I said, laying her down on the deck.

“Didn’t…see it in the…tree. Too late.”

“Let me see,” said the warden. She showed us the back of her arm. About six inches up from her left wrist were two bloodied puncture wounds in the fabric. Warden Davis swung into action, whipping off his belt he wrapped it around her upper arm and cinched it down. “How long ago?” he asked, pulling up her sleeve.

“Half hour…maybe less.”

“First aid kit. Bart, have a look around.” Bart took off toward the upper deck to search in the cabin while his dad took off his shirt, bundled it and put it under Carla’s head. Dad took off his outer uniform shirt and did the same. “What did it look like?”

Carla closed her eyes and answered, “Diamondback or…cottonmouth” and then she turned her head and vomited on the deck, fortunately not in my lap.

“Okay,” said Warden Davis, “we need to get her to a doctor. Peter, I want you to find the keys to this bucket. When Bart gets back I’ll have him take you kids in. You can use the ship’s radio to call ahead for EMTs.”

My mind raced as I stood. Yes, I had to see Carla to a hospital. But shouldn’t we all just get out of there and call in the authorities? "There's no reason any of us should stay," I said. "Dad needs a doctor, too. And we can radio the coast guard to take care of these..."

"You're right, Peter," said my dad. "Bob, take Carla down below deck and get her in one of the berths, I'll drive us in." Bart returned with a first aid kit and handed it to his dad.

"Come on," I said, taking Bart by the arm. "We need to find the keys and get this boat out of here."

"I don't need no stinkin' keys," he said, as his dad lifted Carla from the deck.

"You told me in Cocodrie*, that you didn't know..."

"Googled it since then. Grand Theft Yacht. Let's go." We ran toward the cabin to get underway as Warden Davis and Carla disappeared below deck. Dad kept watch and it was a good thing, not five minutes later several men barreled from the tree line toting AK-47s. Dad saw them and hobbled as quickly as he could to the line and, untying it from the stern railing, tossed it into the water. They leveled their guns and Dad hit the deck as shots rang out.

A lot began happening at that moment. Bart was under the dash at the helm yanking on wires, I was seated in the captain's chair praying for Carla, but jumped from the seat at the report of gunfire and spun to the window just as the men broke into a run across the beach. Bart jumped as well and bonked his head.

"Keep working! *Vite vite*!" I shouted to him. I ran to the cabin door. "Dad!"

"GET DOWN!" he yelled. "Get us out of here." Warden Davis emerged from the hatch as more shots rang out. Dad crawled across the deck toward the anchor line, stood and worked the winch as the warden ducked back into the hold. He must have hit the light switch because several explosions rumbled from below me. The men on the beach hesitated for a moment, probably thinking they were being shot at. The engine roared to life. A shot hit dad in the shoulder and the impact knocked him over the rail and into the water, but he'd gotten the anchor up. The yacht began pulling off the sand.

"DAD!" I screamed and took a running leap over the side without thinking a second thought. Shots were directed at me as a dove. Not having any idea how deep the water was I flattened out for a belly flop. It was going to hurt, but far less than breaking my neck. The men continued firing at the boat as it pulled away, picking up speed rapidly, and I swam for my dad who lay on his back in the water. Reaching him I felt with my feet for the bottom and found it. Blood seeped from the wound in his shoulder and mingled with the bayou forming a spreading pool on the surface.

“Dad, dad,” I whispered.

“I’m okay, son,” he managed, “but you shouldn’t have…”

“I’m here, Dad,” I said cutting him off, dragging him for shore. When I got there the yacht was well underway down the bayou and I looked up to the sight of AK-47s in my face.

Again.

18 KILLER INSTINCTS

It wasn't looking good for us, I'll tell you that. Frankly, I was feeling pretty scared. On a good note our fathers were alive and so was Carla. None of us were dead…yet, and Bart was headed for help. On the other hand, dad had a broken leg and a gunshot wound; Carla had been bitten by a venomous snake and once again some of us were in captivity. My father and I were bound back to back in Thachne's tent and the treasure hunter stood over us cursing.

"You're crazy, man!" I screamed with vehemence. "You shot my dad!"

"Oh, you haven't seen anything yet, boy! And you are *not* going to spoil my party!"

"And what party is that?" my father hissed.

"It's none of your business," Thachne snapped. "We've found what we're looking for and in a matter of minutes we'll be long gone."

"Treasure," I said, "this is all about some stinking treasure."

"You are a smart boy," retorted Thachne. "Too smart for your britches, but you figured it out too late. My men are pulling your boat around now. We'll have Lafitte's—I mean *my*—treasure out of here in no time."

"Jean Lafitte?"

"It ain't the guy from the Capt. Crunch box kid."

"But how? After all these years?"

"I found his map in an old warehouse wall down by English Turn, but that doesn't matter. You are going to die."

"What have you done with Hap Deveaux," asked Dad.

"Why, so thoughtful of you to ask," answered Thachne. "He's been my guide. Do you think I could have navigated these bayous without someone who knew these parts?"

"You kidnapped him?" questioned my dad.

Thachne laughed, "Of course not. I simply offered him a job that paid well. Funny what a little money will do and now I have plenty to buy what I need—even people. Of course, I never paid him and had to, ah, dispose of him." He laughed, "I think the gator found him tasty—Cajuns are kinda spicy."

"You are one sick man," my dad said.

"And *you* are a dead man," Thachne retaliated. A goon poked his head into the tent.

"Boss, we've got the last chest unburied, but we need your help getting it to the boat."

"I hired *you* for the muscle, lunk head!"

"I'm sorry, boss, it's too heavy for the three of us."

Thachne swore. *Who needed to go to R rated movies?* "You just can't get good help these days." Thachne took a cigar out of his vest pocket, bit off the end, spit and lit the other end, puffing clouds of foul smoke into the air. "You know," he said through puffs, "I'm going to enjoy watching you die." He took a drag off the cigar, blew a stream of foulness into the air and turned back to his goon, "Shoot these two."

"My gun's back at the boat, boss."

"Idiot!" yelled Thachne, throwing his hands in the air. "Okay, we'll drag the loot to the boat, but then you come back here and waste these meddlers. I have grown tired of them. Come on!" They turned to leave.

"You're not going to get away with this Thachne," chided my father.

"Oh," said the pirate, turning back, "I think I am. Mexico really isn't all that far away. *Au revoir*.* Or should I say *adios* *?" The men left laughing.

I didn't want to die. Sure, I was looking forward to heaven—no matter how good this life was, heaven was ultimately better. And though I longed to be in eternal fellowship with my creator (which was hard to focus on in this earthly life), I believed I was here for a purpose. I didn't want my dad to die either because I would miss him. Yeah, he rode me sometimes about my perceived shortcomings and placed restrictions on my life, but I loved him. He really did have my best interest in mind.

Mark Twain once said, 'When I was a boy of fourteen, my father was so ignorant I could hardly stand to have the old man around. But when I got to be twenty-one, I was astonished at how much the old man had learned in seven years.' I didn't see my dad as stupid by any means, but, at sixteen, I was growing to appreciate his wisdom and love more than ever.

I had to get us out of this jam.

19 BEST BET

That was my second death threat this year. I don't know, I don't think it was something I was going to get used to. Sweat dripped down my back. The sun had to be nearly full mast in the sky. I don't know if I was sweating because of the rising heat or because of my nerves. Since my palms were clammy, I determined it was my nerves. *Yeah, definitely my nerves*. I had to think fast, but my mind was a jumble of terror. Synapses were firing left and right in my brain. Our situation was serious and I knew it. We were trapped. We were scheduled for execution. We hadn't found Hap and he'd been murdered. The treasure was about to be taken away and these pirates were going to get away Scot-free. *Scot-free. What did that mean, anyway?*

My mind raced through the mega-catalogue of movies stored in the recesses of its gray matter hard drive: *Star Wars*, *James Bond*, *Indiana Jones*, *The Avengers*, *Jaws*,

Crocodile Dundee, *RED* and *RED2*, *The Hunt for Red October*, *The Princess Bride* (of course) and a host of other movies—westerns, sci-fi's, spy movies, even rom-coms. I wasn't getting anything. *Where was inspiration when you needed it? Spies!* Again, I thought back to our tour of CIA headquarters. *Had I gleaned anything useful from what they told us and what we saw?*

Rule number one: Don't get caught. *Well, so much for that.* Disavow who you are. *Was that Mission Impossible or CIA? Both.* Take in everything. Remember the details. *Okay, okay*! *What else?* Be creative. Think outside the box. *That was me.* Weapons training, hand to hand combat. Martial arts. Codes, encryption and ciphers. Languages. Poisons and drugs. Escape techniques. Knowing how to lie. Explosives. *Oh, yeah!* Evasive maneuvers. Computers and communications. Disguises and playing a part. *I can do that.* Clandestine operations. Agent acquisitions. Improvisation. Surveillance. Flying an airplane and parachuting from one. Rope climbing… *This isn't getting me anywhere, brain!*

"Peter," Dad shook my wrists, "got anything?

"I'm getting a jumble, Dad."

"We have to hurry, son."

"I know, I know," I whined, having self-doubts.

"I know you can do it, just think!" He struggled at the ropes between us.

"I am, Dad, I'm thinking too much." *That's it!* The key was the ropes. *Knife. Fire. A shard of glass.* That had worked before. My eyes searched the tent. There were beer bottles, but I had no way to reach them. We were tied to a tent pole in the center of the pavilion. I looked down at the plush carpet on the floor. And then it came to me. In my mind's eye I saw a room with a Persian rug, tapestries on the wall, a large fireplace and two men sitting back to back in chairs at the center of the room.

"Dad! Dad!" I said. "Relax your hands. This might hurt some."

"What are you going do?"

"Just follow my instructions."

"Okay, son. I believe in you." I had a good dad. Sure he could be tough on me. But he believed in me.

"Dad, I think I might want to be a CIA agent someday."

"I think you'd be good at that. Now, let's do this."

'There are some times in life when you fall down and you don't feel like you have the strength to get back up. Do you think you have hope?' The words of Nick Vujicic*, the speaker at Acquire the Fire, came back to me. *'I just want you to know: It's not the end. Are you gonna finish? Are you*

gonna finish strong?' He had no arms or legs, yet with Christ in his life, he had it in him to finish strong. I could do this; I had it in me.

* * *

I didn't know if my new plan would work any better than the last. It was just an idea. I mean, just because it works in the movies doesn't mean it will in real life. You knew that, right? Well, I know that, too, but, hey, I figure anything's worth a shot (especially when you haven't got a better idea). This was our best bet and it came from another of my favorite films: *Indiana Jones and the Last Crusade* (yeah, I liked Dr. Jones). It would be followed, I hoped, by another little surprise based on the movie *Tangled*, Disney's telling of *Rapunzel*.

Since we were back to back we worked at each other's bonds like Sean Connery (my favorite "Bond, James Bond" by the way) and Harrison Ford in the Nazi mansion. It's hard to work at what you can't see, let me tell you, but there was no alternative. *Jesus, make this work*, I prayed.

20 TREASURE!

Working as fast as I could I wedged my thumb under Dad's bonds and pulled with all I had, cinching up the other coils around his wrist while making the loop under which I had my thumb as large as possible. "Tuck your thumb into your palm," I instructed. When I felt him move the thumb into position I pulled the loop down toward the digit. "Now, keeping your thumb as close to your palm as possible, bring it up through the loop."

My father did as I instructed. "Now curl your fingers into your palm." When I felt him do so I worked the rope over each of his knuckles until the loop cleared his hand. "Okay," I said, "it's all yours. Twist the loop and alternate back and forth, looping over your fist until the rope comes free." Within a minute the rope fell slack from his hand and he worked it off the other. He brought his hands out in front of him and untied the bonds from his feet then turned and untied me.

"Well, so much for part A," he said. "That worked quite well, son, though I thought you were going to sever my hand. It's still numb and tingling."

"Yeah, well, now comes the hard part." We rose from where we'd been seated and grabbed some of the heavier books and stood on each side of the tent flap waiting for our elected would-be executioner to return. When he came through the door we would bash his head in with the tomes like Rapunzel did to Flynn with her frying pan, but after five minutes we figured he wasn't coming back and decided to just hightail it out of there. We dropped the books and I poked my head out the opening.

"The coast is clear," I said. "Can you get along?"

"I'll make it. Where are we going?"

"Back to the stash. Grab those beer bottles and put them in that knapsack." I said, pointing. We worked together and gathered the containers from the trash receptacle next to Thachne's desk and left. I helped Dad hobble along and, although he didn't complain, I saw the pain on his face with each step. At last we arrived at the stash. I gave my father the potato cannon as he picked up a limb to use as a crutch.

"Uh, son," he said, "I do believe we left the potatoes back on the yacht."

"We don't need potatoes," I said. "Besides, what good would they do? We're using Molotov cocktails, hence the beer bottles."

"I wondered what you wanted with those. I thought you were recycling." I smirked and handed him the remainder of the rags and the Aim n Flame, instructing him to stuff them in his pockets.

I grabbed some of the beat up flares as well as the butane, stuffed them in my back pockets and picked up the five gallon drum of paint thinner, "You're on your own the rest of the way. I can't help you and carry this at the same time. Can you make it?"

"I will." My dad was such a trooper; I was learning to appreciate him more by the minute. Another ten minutes and we were back at the tree line looking across the shore at the tour boat. Thachne and four thugs were shuttling buckets of doubloons from a broken trunk on the beach to the boat and dumping them onto the deck. A second rotting sea chest lay on the deck, opened, with gold and jewelry spilling over its lip. Other larger articles of gold lay about the deck.

I noticed the trunk on the shore—split open as it was—nearly empty. The men must have dropped it because, even though they must have been working on the transfer for a good ten minutes, Thachne was still swearing and chewing them out as they worked. Their guns were slung over their backs as the carried the booty. I looked at my dad; sweat poured from his face and his shirt was stained with perspiration at the pits, back and chest and with blood at his shoulder. New anger welled in me.

"We have to work fast," I whispered. "Are you okay?" He nodded. "You hold the bottles and I'll pour. When they're full, you stuff rags in the necks while I load the gas chamber with butane." He picked up a bottle and I screwed the lid off the thinner; hefting the container to pouring position I filled the first bottle. My dad sat it down, wedging it into a clump of grass so it would stay upright and picked up another bottle. When we finished the last bottle I took it from him and tried it in the cannons muzzle. It slipped too easily. There was no resistance which meant the gas wouldn't pressurize in the chamber behind the bottle and would leak out as fast as I could fill it. "How many rags do we have?" I asked.

Dad removed the wad from his pocket and counted, "Seven."

"Give me three." He did and began stuffing a rag into the neck of one of the six bottles we'd filled. I handed him the Aim n Flame and took the bottle from him wrapping it in another rag. I wedged it into the barrel. It made snug fit and I began filling the chamber with butane.

“Pete, what if the charge shatters the bottle?”

“There’s going to be an explosion.”

“I know that, you’ll get burned.”

“Let’s just hope the bottle doesn’t shatter then.”

“Let me do the shooting, son.”

“But you’ve never shot one of these. I have the experience, Dad. I can shoot a spud through a tire swing from twenty yards.”

“But…”

“It's not impossible. I used to bullseye womp rats in my T-16 back home,” I said.

“You aren’t Luke Skywalker.”

“But the force is strong with this one. I gotta do this, Dad.”

“I know. Looks like they’ve finished up. Better hurry.” I took aim and prayed. I had three shots and I knew there was a risk. I had to make the first shot count; it might be my only one. *Jesus, protect us.* I steadied the barrel, realigned my aim and, letting out my breath slowly, squeezed the igniter button. WHOSH! The gas ignited and propelled the bottle from the barrel with a pop, the charred rag that had cradled the bottle fell at our feet. The projectile arched over the swampy beach to the horrified stares of the men standing in the boat sixty or so feet away. I didn't even look to see if I was on target.

"Another one!" I yelled and Dad bent over for another bottle and, wrapping it in a rag in one swift motion, handed it to me. I looked back at the boat while stuffing the bottle in the barrel. I saw that my shot had hit the backside of the bow. I recharged the chamber. The water behind the boat was aflame. *It just impacted on the surface*, I thought. The men were scrambling for cover and their weapons. Again I took aim as Dad lit the rag fuse and they leveled their guns. I squeezed the ignition.

WHOOSH! The second shot was off and Dad handed me another cocktail which I shoved in the barrel. I looked up while recharging the chamber for our third and final shot and saw that the bomb had smashed into the center of the boat's wooden seating benches. Flame spread rapidly across the inner hull as the men—one with his pant leg on fire—dove from the boat. In the water now Thachne ordered his goons to splash water into the boat.

"Get the fire out you lunk heads!" he screamed hysterically over and over. I knew that it wouldn't work, you didn't put out a flaming liquid with water.

Dad lit the rag and I fired my third shot. It alighted on the canvas roof which burst into flame, burning chunks dropping into the boat. The men stopped their frantic, inept effort to douse the conflagration and made for the shore. KABOOM! The boat's gas tank ignited in a thunderous combination of black cloud and fireball that rolled skyward. The concussion knocked the men off their feet and they bit dirt—mud actually. I took another bottle and the final rag and stuffed them into the cannon.

"I know I haven't got a fuse but…"

"You can still add fuel to the fire," said Dad, completing my sentence. "I know, but I have a better idea." He removed the bottle from the barrel and put the rag inside its neck. "Here," he said, handing me the bottle and the Aim n Flame, "Charge onto the beach and lob this at the men. Don't worry, their guns are wet now and they're distracted. Go, then run back here as fast as you can."

I ran with all I was worth toward the men. "Get that boy!" yelled Thachne and, when the men began to pull themselves from the mire, I lit the Aim n Flame and touched off the rag, lobbing the bottle toward them. It fell to the beach but didn't shatter. I turned and hightailed it back to the trees as the bottle exploded behind me. I looked back and the goons were on my heels. I reach into my back pocket for a flare, ripped off the cap and stuck it to the starter and tossed it over my shoulder. I don't think it did anything a normal flare wouldn't do. I didn't look back to find out. When I arrived back at the tree line, my father had just finished emptying the remainder of the paint thinner in a swath across the forest edge.

"Give me some fire," he said and I tossed him the lighter. He clicked it on, shoved me behind him and lit the ground on fire. "Come on," he said, pulling me behind him into the woods. He and I staggered along side by side, Dad grimacing with each step.

Flup, flup, flup, flup, flup, flup, flup. I heard the sound, but didn't see the source, but I knew what it was—a chopper. We stopped running. "STAY WHERE YOU ARE. PUT DOWN YOUR WEAPONS." The amplified voice was broadcast from the helicopter pilot. A moment later I heard a strafing of machine gun fire. Dad pulled me to the right and we began an arch back towards the shore. Arriving again at the tree line we took cover and surveyed the situation.

Thachne and his goons lay face down in the sandy mire and duck grass. The chopper sat on the beach, rotors slowing, a Coast Guard SWAT team, guns drawn, surrounding the thugs. We walked onto the beach.

"THAT YOU, MEYER'S?" came the voice from the chopper's speaker. Dad waved as we walked toward the group of captives and captors. We were rescued! I sent up a prayer of thanks.

* * *

The fuel burned up and the fires died down. Only the wooden seats of the aluminum hulled boat still smoldered when a flotilla of boats rounded the bend in the island—a small Coast Guard cutter, a Saint Tammany Parish police boat and a yacht—lit brightly by the climbing sun above the treetops in the east. They pulled up to shore where Dad was speaking with the rescue crew from the chopper. Bart's dad stood on the yacht's deck with a rifle held across his chest and waved to Dad who waved back.

When the boat beached Bart came out from the wheelhouse, waved, bounded down the ladder and sprang over the bow. When he reached me we hugged. Not some sissy hug, mind you, but that manly back pounding guys give one another after a touchdown. *Ouch!* My ribs hurt from the tumble down the boat's stairs and the belly flop into the water.

"You are one sight for sore eyes," he said.

"You ain't too bad looking yourself," I teased.

"What happened here?"

"Whasamattayou?" I said gangster-like. "Wa's it look like? We blowed up da bad guys," I laughed.

"You have all the fun," he mused.

“Come, look at this,” I said, shoving him toward the tour boat laden with gold glittering in the sunlight. I couldn’t believe it! There it was, like Aladdin in the cave of wonders. Except this was the boat of wonders. Gold everywhere! It was like *Pirates of the Caribbean* only, without Johnny Depp.

“Whoa!” exclaimed Bart.

“Yeah, Lafitte’s treasure.”

“No?!”

“*Fo troo*,” I answered, thinking of what Gandalf said in *Lord of the Rings*: ‘All that glitters is not gold.’

21 HOUMA AGAIN, NATURALLY

It took the rest of the day to fill in the authorities back at Slidell City Hall, pick up Carla from the hospital where Dad was patched up and get our friends from the hotel. Reed *had* received our text and contacted the St. Tammany Sheriff about the same time that Warden Davis was radioing in to the Coast Guard from the yacht. Reed, Dallas, Keilah and Beth were all relieved to see us and after much ribbing about Batman a.k.a. the Black Knight, Gator Girl, The Rock and Redeye; lots of hugging; and the reiteration of our adventure, the warden fueled up the van while we got to-go at the Popeye's next to the service station. We set off toward Houma as we chowed down our spicy chicken and jambalaya.

* * *

An hour later Bart's dad drove the van west on 182 into Houma and down West Park to Barrow and turned south. We passed the Cajun Café Dance Hall, sided and roofed with corrugated tin and painted with an alligator enjoying a cocktail. It looked like a *fais do do** was in progress as the parking lot was full and I could hear the faint sounds of a lively Zydeco band wafting out the back door. Man, even though I was wiped out, it made me want to two-step!

"Dudes," said Keilah, "the Scarlett Scoop. I could *so* use some ice cream right now." The nearly square, purple art deco building was on our right surrounded by its wrought-iron fence.

"Oh yeah, oh yeah" sang Bart, dancing Gangam style as best he could in his seat.

"Ice cream it is," said Bart's dad. He put on the blinker and turned at the light and drove around the block, coming in the back side. We clambered out of the van (Dad crutching) and stepped into the small establishment, nearly filling the dining space, and were hit by the intoxicating aroma of freshly waffled waffle cones. The walls were covered with a simulated old-fashioned newsprint and the ceiling, hung with period-looking lighting globes, replicated the old saloons of the 1800s.

A stained glass window spelled out *Scarlett Scoop* over the ice cream cases that wrapped around the walls in an L-shape, taking up half the interior. Colorful bags of old time candy hanging from hooks decorated the place. We wandered across the beautifully tiled floor up to the glass cases and were greeted warmly by the teenage boy behind them. The place was cool in more ways than one. Some ice cream was going to make it even cooler.

"Ladies first," said Dallas, tipping his Stetson and gesturing the girls toward the counter.

"Such a gentleman," said Keilah sidling up to the ice cream cases. "I'll have two scoops of Creole cream cheese in a cake cone." I think Dallas blushed, but I couldn't tell for sure; it could have been sunburn. And yeah, I noticed the alliteration. *So clever.*

"A triple cone for me," said Beth. "Death by chocolate, peanut butter cup and pralines and cream on top, please."

Carla ordered a scoop of red velvet cake on top of a scoop of birthday cake topped with sprinx in a cup. Such a party animal, huh? Bart got his usual, mango sorbet topped with gummy worms in a cup.

"I'll…ah, I'll try an Oil Spill," said Reed. "Oh, wait. Maybe the Lagniappe Pop Rouge. No, no, the Oil Spill."

“Make up your mind, flyboy,” said Dallas. “It took less time for the Alamo to be taken.”

“Oh, gimme both. Gregory Corso said ‘If you have a choice between two things and can’t decide, take both.’ In a waffle cone, please.”

“Who’s Gregory Corso?” asked Bart.

“An American poet,” answered Beth.

“*You* read poetry?” asked Keilah.

“Are you kidding me,” said Reed, receiving his ice cream. “I saw the quote on the Internet.”

“Figures,” said Keilah.

I ordered a double Spiderman in a waffle cone and our dad’s got chocolate sodas. After we all got our frozen confections we each took a seat in one of the red and white striped cushioned chairs at one of the white marble-topped parlor tables to savor our well-earned desserts. Dallas? Oh, yeah, he got a scoop of vanilla.

“What a week!” exclaimed Reed.

“You kin say that again,” said Dallas and Reed did.

“I don’t suppose they’ll be any medals this time,” said Bart.

“You’ve got doubloons! Who needs medals?” said Dallas.

“I don’t think we’ll get to keep those,” said Bart.

“I wouldn’t be so sure,” interjected Dad. “According to Supreme Court rulings just last year, what can’t be legitimately claimed by a government entity, well, its 'finders keepers.' You may be some very rich kids."

My eyes popped, "You're kidding me! I can replace my boat that got blown up in our Voodoo Virus caper!"

"We'll see about that," said Dad, "but, I'm telling you this: the bulk of it will go to your college funds. Right Bob?"

"You ain't just whistlin' Dixie, Jim." Warden Davis turned toward Bart and I, "Just remember boys, '*Where you're treasure is, there will be your heart also*.'*"

Yeah, I thought, *the desire for treasure can really mess you up*. I wanted only to store up my treasure in heaven. "Oh well," I said with a sigh, "I'm just glad we're all back safe and sound, I've got rehearsals starting this week."

"What are you in Pete?" asked Reed.

"Phantom of the Opera."

"The Andrew Lloyd Webber musical?" questioned Beth. "You can't sing."

"That's for sure," said Bart. "He sounds like a wheezing weasel when he warbles in worhip." Everyone chuckled.

"Ha ha," I snorted. "No, it's the non-musical version—a play. I'm playing Raoul. No singing required."

"Well, then I *might* come and see you," said Carla. "You promise, no singing?"

"Cross my heart," I said.

Carla cleared her throat, "And, ahem, who's playing Christine? Hmmm?" she raised an eyebrow. *Ooo, jealousy.* I hoped there wouldn't be any kissing in the show and I'm sure she did, too.

"Uh, Mary Murray."

"Oh, she's cute," said Bart, ribbing me with his elbow and giving me a wink. *Ouch!* Carla seethed and glared and pouted and crossed her arms with a harrumph. *Nice.*

"It's at the Le Petite?" inquired Beth, changing the subject for which I was grateful. "When's it open?"

I nodded. That was the community playhouse in town, which was formerly the original Court House. "Right after school starts."

"Wow," said Reed, "that's kind of like a co-inky-dink."

"A what?" asked Keilah, wiping ice cream from her face.

"He means a coincidence," said Beth.

"Huh?" Dallas lifted his Stetson and scratched his head.

"I mean, like, that haunted antebellum that's the opera-theater we saw in New Orleans. The Davis house."

"How many times I gotta tell you?" Beth turned to Reed between licks. "There are no such things as ghosts."

"Says you," said Reed. "Might be." Beth rolled her eyes.

"There we'ren't no Marsh Monster," said Dallas, "now was there?"

"Might still be," mumbled Reed.

"Thing is," said my dad, "and I hate to tell you this, you know, but the city finally found some renters and..." he paused, "...they swear the place is haunted. Something is trying to drive them out and they want out of their lease."

"Cool," said Reed, "the Davis Playhouse Phantom.

"Sounds like," interjected Bart, "something for the, uh, Bayou Boys to investigate."

"Sounds like trouble," said Carla. "I think Gator Girl will opt out this time."

I puffed up my chest. *Ouch.* My ribs still hurt. "I think I'd like..."

"After the play, Sherlock," said Dad, "after the play's over, and..."

"And then The Rock rolls into another case," said Reed in his best announcer voice.

"Hopefully, not so dangerous," added Bart.

"What?!" I exclaimed. "Danger is..."

"Peter Jackson..."

"I know, Dad, I know..."

"I was going to say," he said, "Peter Jackson 'Danger' Meyers." I smiled and Carla kissed me on the cheek. I was so glad she was okay *and* that she'd gone along on our rescue mission. I don't know what I'd do without her. Or my dad. My real treasure was right here with me.

Thank you, Lord.

GLOSSARY/ENDNOTES

CHAPTER 1

- Parish: What they call counties in Louisiana.
- Voodoo Virus: The first book in the *Bayou Boys Adventures*.
- Bayou: a low laying, slow moving, usually brackish (mix of sea and fresh) body of water.
- Acquire the Fire (see the end of the glossary)
- Harlen Ford sighting of the Honey Island Swamp Monster: http://en.wikipedia.org/wiki/Honey_Island_Swamp_monster
- NOLA: New Orleans, LouisianA

CHAPTER 2

- The Big Easy: Another name for the city of New Orleans (especially the French Quarter).
- Third Day is a Christian rock band: https://thirdday.com/ (You may also watch their videos on YouTube and look up the other bands I've mentioned on the Internet.)

CHAPTER 3

- Honey Island Swamp Tours: http://www.honeyislandswamp.com/

- Cajun: A person of French-Canadian decent, possibly a corruption of Arcadian; also the dialect of the Cajuns.
- Satchmo: Nick name of Louis Armstrong, the great American jazz trumpeter: http://en.wikipedia.org/wiki/Louis_Armstrong
- Pralines: A candy confection (pronounced *praw leans*) of Louisiana made from sugar coated pecans.
- *Baguettes*: French bread
- Zydeco is a rollicking French–Cajun music style.
- Parasol: An umbrella (usually frilly).
- William Faulkner: Pulitzer Prize-winning author, http://en.wikipedia.org/wiki/William_Faulkner
- Rue: Street (French).
- *Padnet*: Cajun term for "friend" of "buddy."
- Spanish moss: A gray moss-like plant that hangs in trees and is related to the Pine-apple, even though it looks nothing like it.
- Live Oak: An evergreen oak; there are several related species native to the South.
- Antebellum: Meaning "before the war" and has come to specifically indicating some-

thing that existed or was built before the American Civil War.

- *Fo Troo*: Cajun expression meaning "that's for sure."

CHAPTER 6

- Ocala Indians: These Native Americans lived primarily in Florida, but also settled in the lower areas of Louisiana. (The Houma Indians also settled in the area.) http://www.ocala.com/article/20030101/OCALACOMHISTORY/101010019
- *Flue de luce*: Literally, "flower of the lily" (French).

CHAPTER 7

- "Why so downcast, oh my soul, put your trust [hope] in God" Psalm 43:5

CHAPTER 8

- *Mouche a fea*: lighting bugs or fire flies.

CHAPTER 9

- "Thy word is a lamp unto my feet and a light unto my path" Psalm 119:105
- David Bowie was a British pop star; he starred (and was totally creepy as the Goblin King) in the movie *Labyrinth*.

- *Bos coya*: the knee-like roots of the cypress trees that grow out of the swamp (Cajun).
- *Gallerie*: The French-Cajun term used for 'porch.'
- Glock: A semi-automatic pistol.

CHAPTER 10

- *Vite vite*: A Cajun term meaning "quickly."
- Blue Man Group: A theatrical-musical group known for their odd performance, bald heads and blue costume and make-up. http://www.blueman.com/

CHAPTER 11

- War of 1812: http://en.wikipedia.org/wiki/War_of_1812

CHAPTER 12

- Yiddish: The High German language of the Jewish people.
- Tuvak: A black Vulcan in the TV series *Star Trek: Voyager*.

CHAPTER 14

- "Let no unwholesome thing come out of your mouth" Ephesians 4:29
- Galley: The kitchen of a ship of boat.
- *Adieu*: French for "farewell."

CHAPTER 15

- Cribbage: A card game (also known as Crib) that utilizes a peg board for tracking points.

CHAPTER 17

- *Cocodrie*: A small town and bayou in southern Louisiana. The name means "crocodile" or "alligator."

CHAPTER 18

- *Au revoir*: French for "goodbye."
- *Adios*: Spanish for "farewell."

CHAPTER 19

- Nick Vujicic: See http://www.lifewithoutlimbs.org/ (You may also view his videos on YouTube.)

CHAPTER 21

- *Fais do do*: Cajun for a dance party.
- "Where your treasure is there will your heart be also" Matthew 6:21

To learn more about an <u>Acquire the Fire</u> youth event near you see: http://www.acquirethefire.com

ABOUT THE AUTHOR

Gregory E. Zschomler is a writer and author living in the Pacific Northwest. He has been married to Ruth for thirty years and has eight children.

This is his second novel for teens though he has published numerous articles and the textbook ***Lights, Camera, Worship!*** He is a theater professional and award-winning playwright, enjoys travel, cooking, Cajun music and food. Oh, and he's a follower of Christ and crazed fan of all that is Disney. Look for him on Facebook or at gregoryzschomler.blogspot.com.

Tell your friends about the

Bayou Boys Adventures

Look for the next book in the series coming Thanksgiving 2013!

PLAYHOUSE PHANTOM

And, if you haven't already, be sure to read:

VOODOO VIRUS

Made in the USA
Monee, IL
09 November 2021

81155171R00095